ANTOINE VOLODINE

The Monroe Girls

TRANSLATED FROM THE FRENCH BY ALYSON WATERS

archipelago books

Originally published as *Les filles de Monroe* in French in 2021 by Éditions du Seuil

First Archipelago Books Edition, 2026

Library of Congress Cataloging-in-Publication Data available upon request.
ISBN 9781962770552

Archipelago Books
232 Third Street #A111
Brooklyn, NY 11215
www.archipelagobooks.org

COVER ART: Marc Giai-Miniet
Typeset by Jillian Kravatz

The authorized representative in the EU for product safety and compliance
is eucomply OÜ, Pärnu mnt 139b-14, 11317 Tallinn, Estonia,
hello@eucompliancepartner.com, +33 757690241

This work received support for translation from the CNL (Centre National du Livre), a public institution that supports books and reading in France.

Archipelago Books gratefully acknowledges the generous support from the Carl Lesnor Family Foundation, the New York City Department of Cultural Affairs, and the New-York State Council on the Arts with the support of the Office of the Governor and the New York State Legislature.

PRINTED IN CANADA

The Monroe Girls

1

For a moment, the girl remained suspended from the ledge that ran along the fourth floor, then she fell and disappeared into the gleaming darkness of rue Dellwo. Her name was Rausch. Rebecca Rausch. Thirty years ago, I was madly in love with her. Then she died.

After the fleeting black streak of her plummet, there was no change in the heart of the night. The colorless image was clear, but nothing was happening there. It had rained. Cold droplets collected on the underside of the electric wires running from house to house; they regularly detached themselves and hurtled to the ground far below, landing on paving stones or in puddles after a brief flicker and, probably, a tinkling sound. The image was fixed, but nothing prevented one from superimposing a discreet soundtrack on it. The plink, plink, plink after the rain. Other than that, no sound enlivened the scene. Two out of three streetlamps were unlit. Not a single light shone behind the windows. In the middle of the road, the tram tracks appeared to be in a wretched state, emerged or submerged according to the hollows and bumps in the ground.

The girl was still there, curled up on the pavement. After five minutes, she stirred.

She was lugging lots of military gear—a front pack, a sawed-off shotgun, a two-way radio—and she was no longer immobile. If anyone had been nearby, they would have thought she resembled a large evil beetle splashing around in the oily mud of night. But no one was looking at her and, when she got to her hands and knees to begin crawling, she shivered from pain, cold, and loneliness.

"Fuck!" she muttered. "I could've easily broken a leg!"

Like many of us, she belonged to an intelligent species, or at least a species intelligent enough to think out loud. Regarding our intellectual activity when we are not grumbling, when no sound escapes our lips, veterinarians and thanatologists disagree. But these quarrels are from another era. In reality, neither language nor thought is necessary to live or survive. Perhaps the girl didn't think all the time, she acted.

And so, she'd already moved away from the spot where she'd landed. She hadn't gone very far. The distance could be counted in meters. Four or five meters maybe. Then six. The girl traveled on the sidewalk, along the bottom of the dark façades. Half standing, half creeping, brushing against the wall. The pools of black water didn't stop her, and her extremities were now wet. The dripping and lapping continued around her. Increasingly she blended into the background. Soon she penetrated a zone of shadow so thick that movement could no longer be detected.

The freezing droplets beat down from time to time on the pavement. They drew an extremely thin and ephemeral silver line and then exploded into the emptiness.

The emergent tracks shone beneath the rare working streetlamps.

The façades turned gray, inanimate.

At the base of the walls were puddles.

And now, in the image of the street, that was all.

2

And once again, the image. The girl remained suspended at the level of the fourth floor, between earth and sky. She had a name. Rausch. Rebecca Rausch.

She resembled, rather than a girl, an oval mass, lopsided and black. Flat against the façade in an acrobatic position, she clutched a relief in the wall that couldn't be distinguished clearly because of the distance and the dark; it seemed to be her only hold. In any case, she held on. She must have had a formidable grip because, in addition to her body weight, she had to support the military gear of a foot soldier or a commando and a field radio as well. She was dangling above the void, motionless, feebly enhaloed by the light of the nearest, very dim streetlamp some hundred meters away. Around her, the windows absorbed all reflections, as if their panes had been replaced by slabs of coal.

Then she let go, speeding toward the ground like a big dark stone, without the slightest gesture to brace herself, soundless.

For a long moment she seemed unobservable. The image was now blurred only by gurgling and the silvery notes that come after a rain shower. The street resembled a rectilinear canyon, sufficiently wide to be veined with a tram's double track, a railway where no wagon had creaked or putt-putted for one or two generations and, in any event, not since the night had begun.

Nothing shone behind the walls. The houses exhibited lifeless black openings, sometimes hidden by blinds whose slats one assumed were heavy with filth. The buildings were connected anarchically by a jumble of wires. They reminded one of footbridges made of vines, or webs woven by giant spiders. It was impossible to know if electricity was moving through the cables. The water of the saturated atmosphere gathered beneath the curves and continually dripped into the puddles, on the sidewalks frightening in their solitude and blackness, or between the half-submerged tracks.

For a few indeterminate minutes, let's say five, the music of the after-rain formed a single soundtrack. Then the girl on the sidewalk emerged from her catatonic state. She herself would have been incapable of saying if her immobility had been due to having fainted, to a normal period of sleep and physical recuperation, or to an emotional shock.

Incidentally, a bit like all of us, she belonged to a species that spoke little, and only in those brief moments when something came to mind.

"Fuck!" she exclaimed softly.

She began to trudge along a wall. A pool of rain had accumulated and she plodded slowly through it. She plowed the water ahead of her as if she were cleaning the sidewalk with a mop.

"Fuck!" she said again. "I was just born, the night is young, and already my feet are frozen!"

3

Next, nothing else occurred, except for a few shudders of black water. The street was just about as frozen as in a photograph. One could make out portions of tracks between the puddles and fog stagnating around the streetlamp, far from the spot where Rausch had lost her footing. Not a single window had been lit, even furtively. No candle, no bedside lamp, no lantern. The darkness of the houses suggested a catastrophic absence of life. Or the predominance of a form of existence too tied to the beyond to feel the need for light, however faint.

After half an hour of observation, the odor of the street—reminiscent of a hospice—wafted up to the bedroom.

I signaled to Breton. He looked at the street in turn, sniffed, and made no comment.

"The girl fell," I said.

"I know," said Breton.

"She left the black space," I said.

"She did it," Breton confirmed. "She's born."

"It was Rausch."

"Rausch or another girl," Breton qualified.

In the gloomy gully that rue Dellwo resembled, the rain had stopped. The water slid along the cables coming and going between the houses without any logic. It dripped down from the rooftops and punctuated the night—with the exception of those multiple and at times melodious plop-plops, there was nothing in particular.

Then, from the depths of the humid murk, the girl reappeared in a corner. It was Rausch, no doubt about it. In particular, one could see she was carrying military gear and bags on her back that weighed down her figure, giving her the appearance of a deformed beast, half asleep and in tatters. She stretched herself to check the state of her limbs one after the other, then shuddered or spasmed and almost immediately set off again. It wasn't easy to follow her movement—it was so far away and in the heart of darkness. She went along slowly, straight in front of her, apparently indifferent to the pooled water soaking her joints and extremities.

"She's going to have a hard time integrating," I remarked.

"I suppose she'll stay hidden for a bit," said Breton.

"Hidden or not, she's going to have a hard time of it."

Just as she paused in her crawling, the girl said a few words. Then she moved forward again and the next moment entered a very dark zone from which she did not reemerge.

"What did she say?" asked Breton.

"I don't know," I said. "It got lost in the dark."

4

Over the years, Breton had sagged and, whereas in his youth he'd had the appearance of an athlete and even the muscular abilities that go with it, now he could pass unnoticed amid a group of seventy-year-olds being led to the slaughterhouse. He turned his jaundiced, withered face toward me, his physiognomy of a mummy. He was standing near the door but had not yet reached for the doorknob. I raised my eyebrows and asked him silently what he intended to do. Without a word, he showed me his pack of cigarettes, wrapped a scarf around his neck, and went out.

I took advantage of this to go drink a glass of water in the bathroom area. The bedroom resembled a shabby hotel room: a bed without linens and a wooden bedspring conceived to host carcasses who had absolutely no claim to comfort. In addition to this particularly narrow cot, there were two chairs, an empty closet, and a small coffee table on which we'd placed a chessboard. Breton was black, and losing. There was also a nightstand. We'd pushed it away from the bed. We placed our observation equipment there when we weren't using it.

As I was about to take up my post in front of the window to try to regain visual contact with the girl, the door opened and Breton came in. He wasn't alone. He was accompanied by two tall guys. I thought I'd already seen them in a general assembly, perhaps they were Party militia men linked to the "Communards of the Highest Awakening" or the "Red Renouncers," two factions of which I'd never been too fond. They looked like gangsters with overcoats that reached down to their ankles, KGB-style. They were wreathed in a nasty scent. Some sort of mixture. Bus station spiders, hotdog stand air freshener. Breton seemed tense and sought my gaze. He wanted to warn me about something. I didn't understand what he was trying to transmit to me.

One of the tall guys shoved him aside and strode toward me.

"What are you doing?" he asked.

For an eighth of a second, I read in Breton's eyes what I needed to answer.

"I'm looking at the rain in the courtyard," I lied.

Since my face expressed incomprehension, the guy came closer to me and pointed to the window. His coat stank.

"You'd better tell us what street you see," the guy said.

"It's raining," I said. "You can't see a thing. Only avenue Chouïgo where the courtyard ends," I said, conspicuously avoiding Breton's gaze.

"There's nothing out there but avenue Chouïgo," Breton confirmed.

We were on the third floor of a ward for schizophrenics. The window was locked to prevent escape or defenestration. The thin wire netting over the windowpanes allowed very little light to filter in. Outside, the hospital courtyard was drenched in black water. The night had become even darker. You could make out a single plane tree, and, a little farther along the avenue, other plane trees and lindens. Rue Dellwo, situated kilometers from there in another direction and in another dream, obviously was not part of the observable landscape.

The guy stood motionless for a second, patently overcome by an urgent need to murder someone. I had the clear impression he was going to plunge his hand into his overcoat, pull out a pistol, and shoot at us. I was paralyzed in turn. The second lasted an eternity.

Then the guy pointed to the optical devices lying on the nightstand—binoculars, night goggles, telepathic vision glasses.

"And what's all that for?" he asked. "To keep an eye on what?"

Breton motioned to the chessboard and cleared his throat. He didn't bother to hide that he was about to say something absurd.

"They're for when we play," he said.

"Yeah," I immediately and insolently confirmed. "To see the pieces better."

Once again, it seemed to me that the militia men were going to gun us down without taking the conversation any further. The guy who was asking the questions had opened his mouth slightly. You could see his teeth clench, his jaw tense. His grimace expressed rage, incredulity, and disgust all at once for having spoken to someone like me. The one who had stayed silent near the door to block a possible escape attempt made a slight gesture, something like a shoulder roll before a brawl. Then they gathered themselves, exhaled, and the talking guy tried again.

"You're going to apply yourself to finding that street, Breton," he said. "Stop with the stuff about the rain on the courtyard. We want to know what street you see. Not avenue Chouïgo."

"And also, what's going on there," the other guy added.

"If there are weird things happening on that street," the first guy reiterated.

"On that too-weird street," the other one declared.

The comment led to a silence. Everyone was trying to imagine the dark street, unknown, with weird things occurring there. The guy near the door pushed the light timer and the central globe lit up, first with a red glimmer, then a sickly glow. It was an energy-saving lamp and, for thousands of hours, it had been saving its energy and diffusing a light for the dying and sustainable development. When we were in this bedroom, Breton and I, we generally preferred the slightly brighter light from the two streetlamps in the courtyard.

"No point staying in the dark," commented the guy, as if to excuse himself for having modified the lighting.

"Do as you're told, or you'll regret it," said the guy next to me harshly, towering over me.

"I don't really see what weird things you're talking about," I said.

The giver of light got aggravated. I suppose he perceived my insolence and was approaching with the intention of threatening or striking me. His spidery, greasy-spoon stench preceded him. It permeated his breath, his clothes, and it preceded him.

"Don't be a wiseass, Breton," he said in a too-familiar, aggressive tone. "I know all about you. And there's nothing good in what I know."

"Bah," I said.

"The Party has looked into your background," he persisted. "They examined it closely. Your file is appalling. Politically, it's nothing but zigzags. Illness can't always be an excuse."

"You're typical of the kind that comes to a bad end," the other man spit out.

They were looking us up and down without trying to hide their disapproval. If they'd combed through the files on us, they must have known that other than my supposed zigzags, I'd never sympathized with their factions. For example, the group "Revenge of the Zeks" or "The Executed to Set an Example," okay, but as for the "Red Renouncers," certainly not. And that, I'm sure, did not motivate them to treat us kindly.

5

"I'm going downstairs for a smoke," Breton said.

He'd twisted a scarf around his neck.

I think I've already mentioned that he didn't have the petulant, dynamic appearance of his youth, and after forty years of incarceration in buildings reserved for the terminally ill, he looked like a man on the decline—let's say a pensioner with a waxy mask—only good for ruminating fatalistically on his past. But obviously, like all of us in the psychiatric kombinat, like everyone subjected to the harassment of the veterinarians and the police, he hid it well.

Alone, I headed toward the bathroom area and urinated, washed my hands, drank a glass of water, then returned to the bedroom. The lamp was not lit. We easily did without it, in any case. The bulb was too weak to dispel the gloominess. I think I already mentioned that, but I'm not sure. I paused above the chessboard. For no reason, Breton had sacrificed a black bishop and he was in a shaky position.

Just when I was about to go back to my spot in front of the window, Breton opened the door with uncommon vehemence. He was flanked by two sinister-looking individuals. They had the look of pathetic Party investigators, of sleazy cops spending their life close to crime or involved in it. I picked up on the warning Breton was sending me from his eyes and, without looking back at him, turned to face his escorts. One of the two came toward me. The second stayed back and barred the door to the landing.

"You're Breton, right?" asked the one heading in my direction.

He was a head taller than me and a torso wider. I suddenly remembered having seen him three or four months earlier at a reeducation session and I think he was already in charge of interrogation back then and was called Strummheim or Donizetti, something like that. Let's say Strummheim. His coat lacked stylishness. He reeked of the strong smells of cheap cafés, cellars, and tegenarie in their egg-laying period. I wanted to vomit.

"So are you Breton or not?" Strummheim threatened.

I nodded.

"Listen, Breton," the guy said in an authoritarian voice. "You're gonna tell us everything you saw on rue Dellwo."

"What are you talking about?" I asked, sounding surprised.

"The street with the tram tracks," explained the one leaning against the door and thus barring the exit.

"I haven't seen a tram in ages," I asserted.

Several seconds of disagreeable tension passed. In front of me, Strummheim had made a slight gesture. His arm had moved upward, perhaps to look for a firearm inside his clothing and point it at my skull, or to burst one of my kneecaps, as cops often do when they want someone to cut short the play-acting and spill the beans.

"There's a house over there that's used as a transit hub. Maybe you glimpsed a girl. What was she doing?"

"A transit hub for what?" I asked, unable to hide my fear.

The guy standing near the door interrupted again.

"What did you see, Breton?"

"Nothing special," I said. "You can't see a thing when you look out the window. The hospital courtyard. The lindens, the plane trees. The night. There's nothing else. If you want to see tram tracks, you have to go to the Baltimore sector. I never go that way. I don't have a permit."

Strummheim shrugged. The odor around him grew stronger. There was something professional about it. Assuming he's not a full-time killer, he must be reeducating the homeless or spiders in cellars.

"And the girl?" he asked.

"What girl?" I retorted in a falsely dumbfounded tone.

Again, the tension rose dramatically. The guy near the door had hit the light timer again and the semi-darkness coming in from outside was followed by the semi-darkness of the energy-saving bulb. Nonetheless I could make out Breton's scrawny shape as it detached itself from our group. He was leaning over the toilet and silently vomiting.

Strummheim went to glance out the window. The landscape was soaked in rain, the courtyard of the Waldemar Ward spewed nothing but blackness. Strummheim passed his hand over the wired windowpane and then, to wipe off his dirty fingers from the dusty condensation, he looked for a curtain and, not finding one because this sort of accessory is absent from the rooms to prevent people from hanging themselves, he changed his mind and grabbed me by the front of my sweater.

"Listen, Breton, vomiting won't solve anything. We've been nice to you. We can become nasty if you try to take us for a ride."

"Very, very nasty," added the other guy.

"We can make you regret you're alive."

"I know. You can."

Strummheim's grip was painful and he wasn't letting go. In addition to my sweater, he was pinching the skin over my ribs. He was hurting me.

"Come clean with everything you know about the girl," he said, shaking me. "Did she show herself? Could you see who she was? Do you know her name? Has she disappeared?"

"What girl are you talking about?" I said. "She neither appeared nor disappeared. I didn't see any girl anywhere."

6

Breton uncrumpled a pack of cigarettes, took one out, and leaned his back against a plane tree. He had found the pack the day before while rummaging through the pockets of a dead man. The tree supporting him had recently been pruned and it raised its stumps above the asphalt, in the shadows, like a sculpture dedicated to amputation in general and of deciduous trees in particular. A gentle rain was falling, not really unpleasant but penetrating, and the spot where Breton had chosen to smoke gave him no protection. He could just as well have stayed three meters from the trunk, exposed to the drizzle from the sky. Yet his shoulders were stuck to the tree. I suppose he was marking in this way his solidarity with the tortured plant and the disgust he felt for what the gardeners had done. He'd stuck himself against the bark and, when he moved the cigarette away from his face, I could see his lips trembling.

In the nocturnal light of the courtyard, the skin of his cheeks, his mouth, and his ears had something jaundiced about them, as if his organism had undergone a sealing or fireproofing treatment, and the treatment had failed.

He waited. Waiting is part of our asylum activity. It's a moment of existence we appreciate and seek out, an occasion to feel slightly disconnected from the disaster, to no longer have the least responsibility for what is happening. That's the stage Breton was at.

And he wasn't alone. Besides me, there was still one of the two policemen who had made us go down into the courtyard, the one who'd fiddled with the light timer. I think I remember his name now: Bourkovine or Biedermann or Bronks. A name that started with a B. Let's say Bronks. We were standing at a slight distance from each other in the silence and the darkness, not saying a word under the lukewarm pall of the rain. Strummheim had left, ordering us not to move. He must have gone to get instructions from some higher-up who was directing the operation from avenue Chouïgo. Or maybe he simply went to empty his bladder in the dark and prostate troubles were delaying him.

The courtyard was deserted and stayed that way for three minutes, then Strummheim reappeared and headed toward us. His face expressed nothing beyond the ordinary brutality and sulkiness of his profession. His dark wool coat was buttoned all the way to the throat. He exchanged a few words with Bronks and drew nearer to us. Once again my nostrils were exposed to the complex odor emanating from him. The mist had modified its components. I started to think about old car trunks and industrial spaces converted into morgues. Strummheim noticed my face tensing. My reactions displeased him.

He began by grabbing the cigarette Breton held in his mouth and tossed it in a puddle at the foot of the tree. If there was a sizzling sound when it hit the water, I didn't hear it. Strummheim had leaned over and whispered menacing words in my ear.

"Easy now, Breton. It's over for you. Stop playing the fool."

The other guy, Bronks, was also very close, scrutinizing me. I would have preferred to hold my breath so as not to notice the stench cocktail coming off him. Tarantula and sludge. I could not hold back a retch and the accompanying sound. Yet I was conscious that at the slightest slip-up on my part, they both would clobber or slaughter me.

"What was that hiccup, Breton?" Bronks panted. "Why are you making those faces?"

"Because I was trying to remember what I'd seen up there when I was looking out the window," I said.

"So, what did you see?" asked Strummheim.

"Nothing," I said. "I was trying to remember, and I remembered absolutely nothing. That's why I made a face."

"You used telepathic glasses," Strummheim said.

"Hirsch glasses," specified Bronks.

"Ah," I said, without agreeing or disagreeing.

"They allowed you to take a look at a street that doesn't exist on any map," Strummheim continued.

"A street with a tram," Bronks said, trying to trick me.

"The tram line is too far away," I said. "If it existed, it would be up north in the Baltimore sector. Five or six kilometers away as the crow flies. Even in a dream, even with the glasses, you can't see much."

"You didn't see much, but you did see something," Strummheim said.

"Someone," insisted Bronks.

He had placed his powerful killer's hand on Breton's bony shoulder.

I never managed to hold out for long in front of the authorities. I'm not a dissident hero. I despise being mistreated and in general I believe that when you play cat and mouse and you're the mouse, it's better to give up immediately.

"Yes," I admitted. "A girl."

I felt, through the claws that were squeezing my collar bones, that Bronks had had the smallest startled reaction. He was satisfied with my answer.

"Well, there we go, Breton," he said. "Why didn't you admit that earlier?"

"Spill it," said Strummheim.

"She fell and disappeared into the darkness," I said.

"Did you recognize her?" asked Bronks.

“Uh, no,” I stammered. “The street is no longer lit. And the Hirsch glasses have defects.”

Bronks removed his hand from my shoulder and shrugged both of his.

“Yeah, right, of course, defects,” he repeated.

He was no longer clutching Breton near his throat but, in one second, he’d become again what he was, a thug clothed in an overcoat like the ones worn by the winners right after a civil war.

We remained motionless for a few seconds, forming a small irresolute group in the courtyard of the Waldemar Ward, near the lone plane tree, under the gentle rain.

“I need to go to the toilet,” I said. “Can I go back up?”

“You’ve already vomited enough, Breton,” growled Strummheim. “It’s not time to empty yourself again.”

I then signaled discreetly to Breton to hang in there and have complete confidence in his sphincters, but in the darkness he didn’t see me.

7

The guys led Breton toward the exit. They didn't utter a single word. They were grim. There wasn't enough rain to wash away their odors.

I didn't know if they were thinking of taking Breton hostage to make me talk in exchange for his freedom, or if they were taking him with them because they were under the obligation to return to police headquarters with a quarry. In any event, they were going to hand us over to a service specialized in interrogation. Strummheim and Bronks were small-time thugs, second-string guys not authorized to conduct an investigation. Apprehending us and frightening us, yes, that was right up their alley, but making us betray what we knew about the girl, certainly not. I say "the girl" as if there were only one, but perhaps it would be better to talk about a whole series of girls. Night after night, they suspended themselves from the ledge of the yellow house, from the fourth floor, and then they let go and fell to the shadowy street near the tram tracks and, after having remained motionless a moment at the edge of the puddles, they readjusted their paramilitary gear, let out a swear word, and disappeared.

We were the only ones to have access to these images, Breton and I. After I don't know what kind of genetic modification, or because during the reeducation experiments we'd had too close a brush with death, or for other obscure reasons, we could see dead people's dreams. We captured them directly on our retinas. The daydreams and adventures of the dead. We could rarely hear their conversations, but we could capture the images of them in discussion. But wait. I'm not claiming that the transmission was constant and without difficulty. The images were often out of focus. But, in short, our information was better than what the police and the Party obtained by other means and, even if they despised us, they had to call on us to learn more.

We had been observing rue Dellwo and the dreams of the same dead man for weeks now, almost every night, and the Services must have known that, thanks to surveillance equipment or informants, or maybe because Breton had said too much during conversations in the cafeteria or the dormitories. We watched Monroe's dreams as if they were screenings of almost-silent films, but in reality, they weren't really silent or repetitive. This visionary ability of ours infuriated them all: policemen, doctors, and Party officials. We were the only ones who could reach rue Dellwo; they had no idea of its location. We were the only ones with the power to visualize the hallucinations or dreams of this man they had executed once upon a time for deviationism. Obviously the Central Committee was worried about this reappearance, this revival. Monroe was among the dead they never wanted to hear about again. Men whom they'd rehabilitated, former Party heroes like Monroe, Oïstrakh, Rozenblat, Mordovienko... The list was long. They had executed them, rehabilitated them, but never wanted to hear about them again.

I'm not much of a political analyst, but I think the Party was still afraid of them, perhaps even more than during those glorious days when it had enough power and malice to get rid of them.

8

We crossed the courtyard on a diagonal. Through the leafy lindens, the streetlamps shed a little yellowish gray. Strummheim and Bronks flanked Breton like hangmen accompanying a guy to the gallows, but then, when they'd passed through the gates, they left him free to move behind them however he pleased, all the while checking that the distance separating them didn't have a tendency to grow. Breton walked without manifesting the slightest desire to rebel or get away, and this docility was sufficient for them.

I followed closely. I had the discretion and the attitude of a lost dog and I overdid the act a bit by stopping from time to time to sniff some tree bark or release a few drops of urine against the walls.

At one time, Strummheim turned to face me. He looked exasperated.

"Breton," he said, "if you keep pissing like that, I'm gonna clobber you."

I quickly zipped my fly and nodded vigorously to express that I'd perfectly understood his threat.

"It just got away from me," I apologized.

Strummheim guffawed contemptuously and began walking again. I drew closer to him as a sign of obedience and, for a good minute, slapped the soles of my shoes loudly on the damp ground so he could hear I'd stopped misbehaving.

We'd left Dadirboukian Square behind and entered boulevard Badbachdaf, passing an endless series of psychiatric wards, dormitories, and treatment rooms. There's almost nothing else in the landscape other than the plane trees on the sidewalks. We didn't come across a soul, whereas often, even at night, patients wander in small silent groups or as solitary sleepwalkers. But tonight, nothing—no lost schizophrenics; we were the only ones walking outside. The rain had been replaced by a tepid fog. The temperature was rather warm and did not justify coats as heavy as the ones Strummheim and his acolyte were wearing. As for me, in my sweater with my neck wrapped in a scarf, I was quite comfortable.

After two kilometers, we arrived in front of an austere building with a dark green granite façade. The building had changed administrations several times over the centuries, but the original inscription had been preserved, engraved in huge letters on a frieze above an enormous door. It indicated that the place had first been a retirement home for cosmonauts and disabled veterans.

There was an indeterminate moment of non-activity, as if everyone were catching their breath before moving on to the following sequence. Breton paused under a streetlamp, analyzing out of the corner of his eye the gestures of Strummheim and Bronks—he was wondering if he would be able to take up his role as vagabond canine again and splash the metal pole. Then Strummheim climbed the stairs, pushed open the door, and entered what appeared to be a thick darkness. Bronks had remained behind. He seemed to be respecting some protocol. As previously in the courtyard of the Waldemar Ward, he remained alone with the prisoner. Strummheim must have gone to announce Breton's arrival to a higher-up. They were waiting to be given the green light to let me go in. This confirmed my notion that our two escorts were mere minions.

Minions. They didn't scare me anymore. What was frightening, because unpredictable, was what would happen next.

9

The door was tall and heavy. Strummheim cracked it open for a second and signaled to us, then let it close slowly. Bronks, not wanting to make an effort because he had a servant at his disposal, invited me to push it. It resisted. After decades of incarceration in the psychiatric camp, Breton had lost much of the strength he could have bragged about in his youth. Above me, the building was enormous, silent, and black.

While I pushed the best I could, using my hip as reinforcement, I thought about this building's history that sometimes Breton, who claimed to know it, would relate. Once upon a time, the place had lodged cosmonauts who'd gone crazy from long exposure to cosmic rays, and invalids torn to pieces by explosions—disfigured, legless, made mad by long exposure to the crimes they'd been ordered to commit. Then, after the apocalypse, Breton claimed, when all communication with space and the front had been cut off, the supervisors waited for the last survivors to vacate the premises. That was when the admission of cancer patients, nurses, and dying idiots began, along with the poorest of the poor—shoved in there out of compassion. At that point, Breton said, after the death of all this scum, the police turned it into a secret center to carry out whatever dirty business the Party asked them to solve, or to bury.

There, in a nutshell, were the thoughts going through my head in the second I was flexing my muscles to push against the door.

And I would have perhaps wished to prolong that second, dawdle a bit, turn back toward the plane trees on boulevard Badbachdaf, breathe in a gulp of warm air, but suddenly I was brutally called back to reality. Bronks grabbed my shoulders and was forcing me to slip through the doorframe, as if to forbid me from returning to the street on a whim. It's true that I'd barely set foot in the entrance hall and I could have done an about-face and run away if I'd had the presence of mind and more courage.

Breton was standing on the marble flooring, depressed and silent, under the close surveillance of Bronks, who was imprisoning Breton's elbow. Strummheim was there, three meters away. He was accompanied by an inspector who had come to greet us. As best as I could make out his features in the half-light, it must have been Kaytel, a morose bloodhound who sometimes snooped around in the dormitories, alone or with the whitecoats or the Party soldiers.

The little group remained practically motionless for a handful of seconds, the time, perhaps, for Kaytel to become aware of the anxious figure of Breton. Then Kaytel said a sentence or two about the very poor lighting in the hallway, the ceiling lamps that long ago had been powerful, but today no longer worked. He was sorry.

"Not a problem," said Bronks. "We're used to the dark."

Breton sighed. He may have been used to the dark, but he couldn't get used to the stench emanating from Bronks. Despite the long time spent in the fresh air of boulevard Badbachdaf, it hadn't dissipated, and here, inside the walls, it returned with a vengeance into Breton's sensitive nostrils.

"These are the original bulbs," Kaytel explained. "They burned out in the last century and they're inaccessible."

"With giant step ladders we could possibly reach the ceiling and change them," Breton interjected.

The three authority figures looked at Breton, as if by speaking he'd broken all the rules of etiquette. Breton immediately withdrew. He was angry at himself for having tried to establish normal relations with Kaytel.

An intense stench of tarantulas and greasy fritters came down on me like a net trap. Around us, the semi-darkness was not too dense, and we could see each other. But, if anyone had asked my opinion about the atmosphere, I would have said it was sinister and that the shadows were distressingly impenetrable.

Anyway, I remained quiet. No one was asking for my opinion.

10

From that moment on, our days were organized according to an immutable rhythm. Our days and our nights. In fact, for us nothing had changed except the locale and a few small details of our daily life. We had toilets at our disposal whenever we wanted, a hot shower at any hour. We could move freely throughout the building of which we were practically the sole occupants, with the exception of the medical control team and the guards who kept us from reaching the street. For sleeping, we had a whole dormitory to ourselves. In addition to our bed, which had all the bedding and linens we needed, there were thirteen other beds with bare box springs. From time to time some lunatics from the neighboring wards would lie down on them, even some who had spent several days wandering through the psychiatric ward and wound up here. They were transitory guests and they disappeared quickly. And of course, an observation room had been reserved for us upstairs, with a chessboard and some optical military devices, a bathroom, and a mattress in case we needed a moment of rest. Breton summed up our accommodations at the House of Cosmonauts by saying that we were like pigs in slop. I had trouble agreeing with him on that one; he was a bit too enthusiastic for my taste. I reminded him that the pigs in question were destined to wind up in the oven and be eaten. He understood my objection but, because he sometimes had flashes of optimistic moroseness, he insisted: "Well, in spite of that, perhaps we can hide and they won't find us under the slop."

Leaving aside the slop and the oven, our existence was governed by a certain number of disagreeable events. Our life was not as comfortable as all that when you think about it, when you really think about it. We were under constant surveillance, we were shoved and manhandled whenever we approached the exit, we were summoned every two or three days before a committee of whitecoats who stuffed us with drugs and injected us with stuff. And obviously we had to speak with Kaytel on a regular basis.

Kaytel didn't wear a white coat and often kept his trench coat on to interrogate us. I was afraid of his brutality, but less disturbed by his odors than by those of his minions. A trench coat or an overcoat, depending on the weather, but in any case a long, heavy coat. But what I want to stress here is that, although he could smell of damp and tobacco, he did not exude memories of underground passages, pools of black oil, and abandoned butcher shops. Greasy spoons where bushy rodents wind up as hideous kebabs. Kaytel emitted the odors of a commander. Whereas the stenches of a netherworld floated around Bronks and Strummheim.

Officially, I think we'd been transferred to the House of Cosmonauts as volunteers for experiments linked to space-time travel but, in reality, we had wound up in the hands of one of the Party's secret structures. I say "we," but Breton was not always with me, and often I found myself alone, face to face with Kaytel to report my observations of the previous night.

When I entered the House of Cosmonauts, I'd feared being immediately broken into a thousand pieces, but my fears were, at bottom, groundless. Kaytel wanted me to collaborate on the file he'd opened on Monroe. During our first session, I neither admitted nor denied that I could visit Monroe's dreams. But after a few slaps and punches, I'd changed my tune. The Party knows everything, or almost everything, and it was in this "almost" that I'd taken refuge. Kaytel incessantly reminded me that I was the only one able to approach Monroe, the only one with access to the images that went through Monroe's mind. At that point, I had to agree. Yet I emphasized the extreme difficulty of obtaining clear images and the impossibility of putting a date on the dream that had been communicated to me. That's where I had a little leeway. I didn't hesitate to dive into it. Breton did the same.

Kaytel, and with him the entire Party no doubt, and the police, and even the veterinary services, were uncertain about our status in the House of Cosmonauts. I admit that we ourselves were unclear about it. Kaytel attached no importance to our role as guinea pigs in a teleportation experiment listed on the residency permit we'd been given when we entered the building. He didn't believe it and neither did we. The healthcare workers who examined us did so more to check that our bones hadn't been broken during interrogations, and no expert or trainer in dematerialization had come to give us basic advice on cosmonautic magic. Kaytel had dropped the term "guinea pig," totally ignored what was written on our laissez-passer, and, if he often alluded to our status as nocturnal travelers, preferred to treat Breton as if he were one of the living dead, a former zek, or an eternal loser. Above all I think he thought of us as stoolies of bizarre, inferior quality. Stoolies, informants—because he needed us to investigate this Monroe, this individual whose actions, he said, threatened the Party and its future, and even perhaps the future of all humanity.

The future of the Party and of all humanity. So he said.

I knew that the psychiatric compound was the only place in the world still standing, and no one there could escape intense and occasionally persistent bouts of delirium, and I'm not just talking about the imprisoned patients, I'm talking about the police and doctors as well and, of course, the Party survivors. Monroe's key role in the end of History seemed like a crackpot hypothesis to me but, deep down, I wasn't shocked by it. I was inclined to adopt it as if I'd thought it up. It was in keeping with my mood and, in addition, I was flattered to be counted among the saviors in what seemed to be a vast rescue operation of the human race and its last representatives. Finally I had a task to carry out other than the one that consisted of waiting to be locked up in a ward for dangerous animals, or killed. That's why I obeyed Kaytel without balking or asking for additional explanations.

"You're an odd duck, Breton," said Kaytel. "It's a hell of an adventure to be forced to use you in order to learn more about Monroe."

Oh, that made me proud!

"That we are obliged to count on a whack job like you," he specified.

The term "whack job" seemed to lack scientific rigor, but it would have taken more to deflate me.

11

Nothing changed, like I said. A routine existence. Every three days, the minions took us to boulevard Badbachdaf for a half-hour stroll, just the time for two roundtrips during which we remained within sight of the House of Cosmonauts without ever leaving the neighborhood. Breton took advantage of these walks to place his lips on the trees. He whispered apologies and lamentations against the bark, dusty or damp from the rain, until the minions tore him from his prayers. Back at our base camp, before the interrogations began, they fed us on gruel and watery mash as was recommended for the general population in quarantine and the village idiots.

Breton, who had never been very enthusiastic about collaborating with the powers that be, retreated into periods of silence. Kaytel felt obliged to shake him up and, rather than handle the beatings himself, preferred to call to the rescue duos of minions, guys whose identity and techniques we now knew. Bronks and Strummheim, Petrov and Molinari, Park and Browniev. Because these sessions took place in an area that was originally a bandaging room, our torturers were keen on donning white coats, which gave them a nurse's respectability and masked their pestilence, for which we were grateful. Kaytel stayed in the room, obviously, gathering whatever was useful from our moans.

Breton always wound up cracking, but he rarely said the name Monroe and never that of Rebecca Rausch. If he had to denounce girls, he denounced other ones.

When I think about it, nothing changed because nothing could change. There was something fundamentally flawed in the dialogue between us and the police, something that always made it unproductive: on the one hand, Kaytel wanted information, but he lied, he didn't tell us what his intentions were in interrogating us about Monroe, what he really wanted. And, on the other hand, for our own personal reasons, we hid from him almost everything that could have satisfied his curiosity.

12

The Party experts had placed excellent equipment at our disposal: Maliavine binocular masks, Kosch magnifying lenses, anti-glare cloths, and trifocal lorgnettes. We didn't care for these sophisticated gadgets but, out of consideration for Kaytel, we would use them on occasion, going so far as to claim they were helpful to us. In truth, we had no need of them and, with simple Hirsch telepathic glasses and a lot of patience, we could capture what we were interested in more easily.

As midnight approached, Breton would set up the pieces on the chessboard in anticipation of those moments of nighttime emptiness when we would need to hang on to reality, to the concrete moves of bishops, queens, and knights. Then we would shut off the light and glue ourselves to the window, with or without optical devices, for hours. Until the boulevard Badbachdaf that ran along the House of Cosmonauts disappeared. Until in the distance appeared the image of rue Dellwo. The tram line, the miserly lighting, the somber succession of façades and among them the house from which Monroe's girls were born, suspended from the fourth-floor ledge.

Breton often got black in chess, even though we always flipped a coin and never cheated. I usually played white, which didn't prevent me from losing more often than I should have. We were equally good but, in the dark, the

Hirsch glasses offered an advantage. He didn't take them off to analyze the pieces' positions. They allowed him to see, without effort, a half dozen moves in advance.

The stakeout nights were all alike.

Hours of frozen idleness in front of the window. Sometimes we broke up the wait by walking around the room to stretch our legs, or by changing optical devices for no reason, attaching to our forehead, one after the other, the elements that made up the Party's cutting-edge accoutrements: the drill bit with oneiric bubbles, the Korighane visor, the lorgnettes and masks. Sometimes we would even boogie around the mattress, gesticulating like a clown, so grotesque did all this equipment seem to us compared with our basic shamanic gear. We didn't speak other than to announce a castling, a check, or a checkmate. Then, without warning, an image would appear, often extremely clear. Rue Dellwo, on the ledge of Monroe's house, a girl in military garb would begin the journey that would lead her inside our camp.

Then, when we had exhausted the image and dawn came, we would put away the material, go down the hall of the House of Cosmonauts, and, if Kaytel was already there, we would make our report to him. If the interrogation didn't go on for too long and if, next, the veterinary commission was contented with giving us a shot without even taking our blood pressure, we could be entirely free until the evening.

Kaytel would have liked for the investigation to move more quickly and he suspected us of not telling him everything, without, of course, having any proof. His intuition was good because, even if I was generous in my descriptions of Monroe's dreams, I kept to myself the names of the girls and everything concerning Rebecca Rausch. The lack of results infuriated him and, when he could no longer restrain himself, he asked his goons to beat the crap out of us. Those guys knew how to hit, and they would stop from time to time to allow Kaytel to formulate questions, but our sniveling answers added nothing significant to the file.

Over time, I wound up understanding what, more than anything, was bothering Kaytel and the police.

Monroe, who'd found himself in the shadows after having been eliminated, was now suspected of having formed a task force over there in order to resurface in broad daylight with the insane idea of storming the Party, ridding it of its incompetents and its traitors and, in sum, reorienting it toward something other than an ignominious and definitive disappearance. The camp authorities had somehow been informed of this project, but they had great difficulty imagining how it would be carried out. When they learned of the existence of a street that wasn't on any map, with extremely disquieting girls who used it as a transfer hub, they panicked. The police were trying to gather information so that the Party would know how to act. Kaytel was the commanding officer in charge of the investigation. He was leading it in various directions, but we were just about his only reliable source.

Frequently he would unburden himself to Breton. Laid low by insomnia, frustration, and the absence of a future, he would unburden himself. Sometimes I had the feeling I was listening to a patient plagued by depression.

"You understand, Breton?" he'd say to me. "No point drowning in wishful thinking. Nothing good will come from these girls. They're used to living over there, with Monroe. In a dead man's dreams. In dreams and over there with the dead. They'll never see the difference between us and the stiffs on the other side. Don't you think?"

I demonstrated my agreement by puffing my lips and nodding my head two or three times.

With that, he went on. His big obsession was the Party. The Party was in sad shape, and it was even nearing its terminal phase, but the help that the dead wanted to bring it from outside seemed more dangerous than useful. People like Monroe, Zakharov, Pfimster, Oïstrakh, Rozenblat (and a handful of other lesser-knowns who'd been bumped off during the purges)—no way would anyone open the camp doors to them, let alone their battalions of girls who'd stop at nothing.

"We're sick and tired of these factions come out of nowhere," Kaytel explained. "There are already enough here. No need for the dead to invite themselves in to give us advice or a helping hand."

I swayed from one foot to the other. I'd never thought there were too many factions in the Party. True, I belonged to several factions at the same time and, in particular, to an ecumenical and tolerant faction—"The Marxists of Great Compassion"—my favorite. It was a secret faction and it would be ill-advised to claim my adherence to it in front of a cop, obviously.

"By the way," Kaytel interrupted himself. "What about you, Breton? What faction of the Party are you a member of?"

"The Proletarian Samurais," I declared immediately and confidently.

Kaytel would slap me or sigh noisily.

"You're lying," he decided.

And he would slap me again. In general, he had no faith in what I reeled off when I was with him.

Another session, another conversation, I'd spout something else. There was no lack of choice.

"To what faction did you tell me you belonged already?" Kaytel asked.

"The Libertarians of the Incarnation," I proclaimed. With such warmth that even I had the impression I was telling the truth.

"Never heard of it," remarked Kaytel with scorn.

He shrugged.

Often, everything pointed to the fact that he craved giving up the whole business and leaving me to rot in the House of Cosmonauts. Or beating me to eliminate physically some of his despair. A very, very strong craving.

II

13

When he wasn't digging around in the middle of Breton's lies at the House of Cosmonauts, Kaytel worked, or pretended to work, in his office in the Cornelius Ward, not far from boulevard Badbachdaf. It was a place where he was comfortable because he was the sole occupant and could snooze, dream, and ponder the end of all hope without being disturbed by visitors. The Cornelius Ward had been requisitioned by the police, who transformed it into a discreet police station from the center for psychiatric emergencies it had originally been.

Had he so wished, Kaytel could have set himself up on the second floor where the rooms were bigger and better lit but, at the time he'd taken possession of the locale, he'd preferred this medical setting that looked directly onto the courtyard, with its bookshelves collapsing under piles of files and medical journals. He'd liked the décor. I said requisitioned, but in fact there had been no violence or dispossession of any kind. The ward was empty, the medical personnel had abandoned it four or five years earlier. The notion of emergency was no longer pertinent. Patients were no longer flooding into the camp, not because mental illness had decreased in the outside world but simply because in this outside world there was no one left. Almost no one. The police and the Party were in charge of what remained of the living and the organized and, at bottom, since the camp was fairly large, that was already a lot.

Kaytel was overwhelmed at the thought of the responsibilities that fell to the Party and the police, two institutions that, over time, had wound up merging. Overwhelming was the fact of having inherited the sacred values of the world revolution while the existing world had shriveled to the point of being no more than an insane asylum, a minuscule corner of the globe. Overwhelming was the reality of the collective end. Overwhelming was the blindness of the Party officers who, against all logic, were still counting on mobilizing the masses to ensure conditions for better survival. Overwhelming and idiotic was the idea that nothing had failed forever, nothing was doomed, and that it was normal for the police to continue to take on the duties of order and hope. So, since the dead wanted to add their two cents to the last long march of History, because guys like Monroe wanted to intervene from the beyond, Kaytel felt very, very tired. And rather than work, he spent all his time pretending to think.

That's what he did most of the time, on the ground floor of the Cornelius Ward.

14

He took a cigarette from his pack and placed it between his lips. It stuck there as if he'd already drooled on it for quite a while. Then, in order to reach the pants pocket where he'd shoved a lighter, he stretched out on his chair then sat normally again, bringing the lighter toward his face. The wheel rolled under his thumb—an agreeable, almost voluptuous sensation, and a familiar, agreeable noise. The feeling was there, with the sound and smell of the flint, but no flame emerged. The lighter had run out of fuel the previous day.

Kaytel turned toward Dame Patmos, the Party official. She'd just entered the room.

"Would you have a light?" he asked

The cigarette was dancing in front of his mouth, which accentuated his unkempt look that was somewhere between a mafioso, an off-duty cop, and a bum. He liked that style. One hundred and fifty years earlier, when there were still movies shown in dedicated theaters, you could have said he resembled those crooked detectives during prohibition. But today cinematographic culture had disappeared and, as a result, with his look of a fifty-something guy from the trashcans, it would be more accurate to say he resembled nothing.

The glow of dusk filtered in through the windows that overlooked the courtyard. It was raining. He cut a rather pathetic figure in the dying light.

"I quit smoking," said Dame Patmos.

The reason for Dame Patmos's visit was not surprising to Kaytel. The senior official of the Party had had enough of reading reports sent by lackeys and had come to gather the information on Monroe's file herself. It was an investigation that the Central Committee was following step by step with growing hysteria. The lack of results, the lack of progress, the impression that the late Monroe and his bizarre girls were going to set off new catastrophes in the psychiatric camp, in what remained of the world, the impression that the very outlines of the threat were ungraspable—all of this put the Party's higher-ups in a very bad mood.

It also prompted the supreme apparatchiks to question Kaytel's management of the problem. For weeks now, the Central Committee was thinking of removing him from his functions, despite his reputation of being the best among us, at least when you took into account the small number of commanders still not inside padded cells, drunk tanks, or coffins. Which is why, on this day, at the end of this afternoon, Dame Patmos wasn't there on a simple social call. She had a mission. She had been instructed to wake Kaytel from his professional torpor, and if that seemed impossible, she was to fire him, or even execute him—she had clearly been given this power. What the Central Committee was unaware of was that this evening, she was ready to tell Kaytel that her long period of widowhood had ended, and that she was once again available for emotional, sexual, or other adventures.

Dame Patmos and Kaytel had been lovers fifteen years earlier, rather passionately but fleetingly and, even though they'd gone their separate ways, they'd left each other on good terms. Without having completely lost sight of one another, they'd had few occasions to stay in contact for they had not followed the same path. People looked askance at Kaytel. His individualism was offensive, as was his nostalgia for obsolete factions such as "The Mothers of Late Night" or "The Leninist Church of the First Day." His superiors appreciated his bitter lucidity and his taste for secrets but, even if they sent him into theaters of operation that demanded common sense and few scruples, they were in no hurry to acknowledge his successes. Sometimes he even sensed that the authorities were waiting for him to fail utterly in order to get rid of him. After fifteen years of service, he hadn't committed any major blunders, but he hadn't made much progress either. Whereas Dame Patmos had climbed up through the Party ranks, thanks to what could be called her petulance combined with an incontestably ideological steadfastness. She'd been promoted years ago to the secretariat of the Executive Committee and today she had the look and the mindset of a huge bureaucratic cow.

They had not followed the same path and, in any case, as far as love was concerned, everything had to start again from scratch.

"Oh, I hadn't noticed you'd stopped," said Kaytel with some surprise. "I thought you'd never manage it. You always said you didn't give a damn about lung cancer."

"And I still don't," said Dame Patmos. "I only stopped a week ago. It makes you put on weight."

She sat across from Kaytel, in the visitors' chair. It groaned under her considerable bulk.

"A week isn't very long," Kaytel commented.

Dame Patmos smiled broadly, showing her strong, white teeth. Kaytel returned her smile. Despite her excessive plumpness and her more than fifty years, she was still attractive.

She opened the bag swinging against her shoulder and, after five seconds of exploration, withdrew a small matchbox decorated with a naïve illustration like the ones that were still made three centuries earlier in the Second Soviet Union. She held it out to Kaytel, hinging forward. Stuffed into a blue military-style suit, flowing out of a white blouse with a few buttons undone, her breasts blossomed forth.

"But here you go. I still have a light for my honey," she said.

Kaytel grasped the box, looked at it with some emotion at the thought of the Second Soviet Union, opened it, cracked a match and, as the tip of his cigarette was already glowing, put out the flame by shaking the match.

"Don't call me honey," he said, exhaling a stream of dense gray smoke.

"Why? Does it bother you?" chuckled Dame Patmos softly as she took back the matchbox.

She'd sat down again. A bureaucratic cow, torso erect, harmonious though somewhat puffy features, luscious lips, well-groomed eyebrows, clothes of a paramilitary officer—dark blue with a touch of shiny sequins, severe blouse that nonetheless didn't hide any of her opulent bosom that invited contemplation and stroking. She cast a glance—a blend of intelligence and sensuality—at Kaytel.

Without answering, Kaytel exhaled a second puff. Over the last fifteen years, he'd given up on all the passionate ways and byways of his youth, as well as on all official political beliefs. It was difficult for him to conceive of a better future for our great-grandchildren and those of others. He knew the human species wouldn't get that far and, in order to accept this awful perspective, he'd had to harden himself. All of a sudden, the thought of his love affair with Dame Patmos pitilessly reminded him that he'd grown old, that he'd lost faith, and that everything was screwed.

Because he didn't answer, Dame Patmos persisted.

"You don't want to be reminded of your former loves?" she asked.

"That's all finished," said Kaytel.

"Nothing's stopping it from starting again," simpered Dame Patmos.

"We're too old," said Kaytel. "It's over."

He vaguely, almost dreamily, recalled his comrade's body as he used to palpate and penetrate it half a generation earlier, those few moments of embracing, of exquisite excitement. A few orgasms in the psychiatric wards that were used as motels. For a quarter of a second, he was overwhelmed with melancholy, then nothing.

"Oh, you," Dame Patmos said, scowling.

She put the matches in her bag and looked Kaytel in the eyes. She knew that, if she were to be diplomatic, she should not stop simpering; nonetheless, she'd scowled.

Kaytel avoided her glance. He lowered his head, seeming to say that from now on nothing in life was of any importance. Then he took the cigarette from his mouth and became absorbed in the sorry consumption of his tobacco.

Despite being well over the hump of fifty, Dame Patmos remained attractive. Her face had grown wider, her flesh swollen, but the harmony of her features and even the lascivious proportions of her body had changed accordingly and today were still practically intact. The excess fat barely erased the memory of the radiant thirty-year-old woman she had been. She had metamorphosed into an enormous female mammal of fifty, voluptuous and still at ease with herself. She was aware she still had seductive powers if she put in some effort. And she did.

The two of them remained facing each other without a word for a long moment, like in a Taiwanese movie under terrible French influence, or like in a post-exotic tale right before a scene of criminal violence. Outside, the rain sputtered in the courtyard and occasionally on the windows as well when the wind blew from the north. The light continued to fade. Soon it would be night. In conformity with Party recommendations for conserving energy, Kaytel didn't light any lamps. He seemed indifferent to the encroaching dusk. Smoke came out of his mouth, forming swirls whose twists and turns were ever more difficult for him to follow. It stank more like fodder than tobacco, that smoke.

"We could begin everything from scratch. It simply depends on you," Dame Patmos said out of the blue.

She couldn't hide a slight tremor deep within her voice.

"What about Monroe?" Kaytel objected.

15

During her affair with Kaytel, Dame Patmos had met Monroe and fallen into his arms in a way that seemed impetuous, exaggerated, and hurtful to Kaytel. Having broken up with Kaytel, Dame Patmos had then begun to live her love life in an entirely public way, a romance admired by everyone who knew her and one that could have taken its place in the long list of fabled love affairs, alongside Bonnie & Clyde or Kurt & Ingrid. In any event, the couple was a joy to see. Dame Patmos had insisted on making the relationship official. She'd married Monroe as much from love as out of careerism—at the time Monroe had been noticed by the Central Committee and some people considered him to be a rising star in the Party. In reality, stellarly speaking, Dame Patmos's husband didn't have time to rise very high. He'd been a victim of the purges during that awful year when the Party was eliminating the so-called anti-Party factions that numbered in the dozens. His disappearance had been programmed and, officially, he'd died in a road accident, suffocated and burned by an avalanche of tar from a tarring machine that he'd rammed straight into while trying to escape the investigators. The circumstances were atrocious as well as bizarre, because already at the time there was no traffic and most often even the leaders went about on foot. In addition, the roads were not maintained, and the tarring machines were no longer in use anywhere. Regardless. Dame

Patmos had then begun to be known as a figure of an inconsolable, incorruptible, and politically inflexible widow. She'd started to get fat, then climbed up the organizational ladder step by step. At first, the shadow of martyr Monroe had been of use to her, because after the purges, the Party had taken a new turn and was rehabilitating the purged. Subsequently her rise had been due to her own merits and the subtlety of her maneuvering. Today she was well-positioned within the Central Committee, responsible for intelligence and for several unmentionable activities the existence of which the Party had thenceforth acknowledged. For example, the protocols for alliances with non-human species, the cries for help addressed to extraterrestrials, or the introduction of black magic into police investigations.

"Monroe is dead," Dame Patmos said.

After several seconds of intense reflection, as if he'd had to prepare a complex synthesis before opening his mouth, Kaytel said, "Yes, that's the problem."

Dame Patmos pouted.

"He's between us," Kaytel added.

"Bah," Dame Patmos protested. "I don't know which Monroe you're talking about. The one who was executed has no place in my life at this point. That's in the past. And you know it."

"He'll always be between us," Kaytel insisted. "He was killed under abominable circumstances. His charred corpse will rise up between us all the time."

Dame Patmos moved lithely on her seat with the unctuousness of a seal. She gently brushed the front of her chest. She crossed and uncrossed her legs. Her seduction enterprise seemed to be off to just as bad a start as the Monroe business.

"I'm not asking you for anything," she said, not without feeling obliged to smile broadly.

Kaytel swallowed one last puff. As he was stubbing out his cigarette, he imagined a bedroom scene, perchance tonight, in his bed, with he and Dame Patmos as the actors. They both knew their roles and were playing them fairly well, relaxed and making the best of things. The male role was played by a fiftyish man with a skeletal body who was immediately out of breath and dripping with sweat. In the female role we had the obese body of Dame Patmos, with her flesh flowing over the sheets, her insolent laugh, and what lay between her thighs impossible to find among all the folds in her skin. This image of their copulation seemed so improbable and so undesirable to him that he kept it short.

"We've always been good friends," he declared. "Let's let it stay that way."

Dame Patmos swallowed her disappointment.

"Why, of course," she said. "Why shouldn't it?"

Her survival and progress inside the Party had taught her that it was better never to say aloud what one was truly thinking, and never really to feel what was happening deep inside, especially when it had to do with sorrow and pain. Thus, the evocation of their friendship was enough to satisfy her for the time being. She leaned back on one of the visitor chairs and for several seconds looked with interest at the décor in which Kaytel worked: the naked walls, the mounds of files and, farther away, the rain dripping down the windowpanes.

Then she dug into her bag and pulled out a cigarette. Thus ended her week of abstinence. She struck a match, brought the flame toward her face, and exhaled her first puff.

"By the way," Kaytel said to break the silence. "Where did you find your matches?"

"There aren't a million places," said Dame Patmos. "Same goes for lighters. You find them by searching the pockets of the dead."

"I guess so," sighed Kaytel. "That's the only place left."

16

Night had fallen now.

Kaytel and Dame Patmos let the darkness permeate the office. They remained face to face, smoking without a word. They had countless subjects in common to contemplate in silence, and they did so freely. They rehashed old memories and young anxieties, new anxieties that had appeared with the menacing advent of the Monroe girls in the camp. The investigation assigned to Kaytel, the meager communication between the real world and the world of the dead that Breton had established, the absence of certainty about the future, the irremediable slide of the Party toward the void, the end of humanity: they dredged up all that, expelling not a word, preferring the tepid drifts of smoke to language.

Then the thunder rumbled nearby and Kaytel, whose back was to the window, glanced over his shoulder. The rain intensified. The streetlamps that should have lit the courtyard of the Cornelius Ward were slow in emitting an appropriate glow. All was black: the sky, the courtyard, the hospital, the room itself.

The downpour spat against the windowpane. A burst of lightning lit the clouds somewhere beyond the quarters of the mentally ill, far to the north.

Then a draft caused the office door to open. From outside the scent of wet leaves drifted in.

Dame Patmos stood up to close the door. Kaytel abandoned his contemplation of the outside scenery to follow her with his eyes. He'd been distressed by the boudoir scene that had cropped up in his mind earlier, and he forced himself not to undress Dame Patmos mentally, to look at her as she was, in the weak light and in the present. His intention was good, but the result was no less distressing. Dame Patmos had the slippery mobility of a female grizzly and, even if Kaytel judged her to have an abnormally fat body, objectively he had to acknowledge her undeniable grace and the fact that she seemed in no way handicapped by her excess weight. Grizzly or not, in her dark blue pseudo-uniform of a Party official, she had class. During this quick moment of observation, while she was going to the door fighting against the wind then turning around, Kaytel enveloped her in an admiring gaze. To hide his embarrassment, and also no doubt so that his admiration did not turn into some form of desire, he removed another cigarette from the half-crushed pack languishing in his chest pocket.

Dame Patmos had just sat down across from him again. Her smile could be made out in the thickening shadow.

"So, you're having another one," she stated.

She again dug into her bag and handed him the matchbox.

"Thanks."

Kaytel exhaled a plume of smoke of no discernible color toward the ceiling. Outside the streetlamps were doing their best, but the bulbs would take another fifteen minutes before reaching their maximum output. Kaytel and Dame Patmos could barely see each other inside the room. The relatively clean, crisp scent of wet leaves that had entered the office a moment earlier had already dissipated, replaced by the stench of a vegetal mixture of dried mushrooms and moss, a stench barely related to that of tobacco, and worse. It had been ages since you could find real tobacco, even by rummaging through the rags of the dead.

"I don't want to make you waste your time. You seem to be drowning in work," Dame Patmos joked.

"Not at all. I'm happy you're here," said Kaytel in a fatalistic voice.

Dame Patmos reached over to retrieve the matchbox Kaytel had placed on the table and, as Kaytel's hand had remained near it, she leaned forward slightly to brush against it tenderly.

"Well, that'd really be something if my presence didn't make my honey happy," she said, withdrawing her hand. And then she let out a not very natural laugh.

She hadn't resisted the desire to go on the offensive again. Ever since she'd entered the office, the idea of a fling with Kaytel had become uppermost in her mind. She felt an irrational desire to fan the flames of their brief youthful passion, to reignite them or, at the very least, to see what she could obtain by fanning them. Although she gave the impression of being a sensual, licentious creature in love with physical pleasure, she had been quite well-behaved during her long and courageous rise to the Party summit. Those had been chaste years for her, and she'd been rewarded with some one hundred extra kilos and admittance to the Central Committee. And now: inner flame. She wanted to seduce Kaytel, to seduce him again. The desire had come out of the blue, as soon as she'd entered the room; it had taken her by surprise, even though she'd thought about it several times the day before and on previous days. It was very strong, and it blazed.

But not so much as to incinerate her duty as Party delegate on a special mission.

"So, where are you in our investigation?" she asked, changing the subject in order to return more easily to the emotional sphere afterward.

The rain lashed at the dark window. Kaytel stood, went to press the light timer and grumble something against the Party's ecological turn. A tube flickered feebly on the ceiling, then another. Inside the office, the light remained pitiful.

"We're getting there," he promised, raising his eyes toward the burgeoning fluorescence.

He remained silent for a few seconds, looking for the right words.

"Breton is in decline," he said in the end. "Personality dispersal. Recurring delirium. Pathological secretiveness. I'm sure he knows where the girls are hiding. They're already in the camp. He's been distracting us with a non-existent street since the beginning. He's like a dog with a bone. We can't count on him."

"So, where do *you* think they are?" asked Dame Patmos.

"Hard to say," Kaytel sighed. "They must have already slipped in among the medical personnel or the patients. They're lying low. They know how to assimilate. They're dangerous."

"They're dead," said Dame Patmos. "The Party is pissed that we can't manage to locate them."

"They're no more dead or less dead than we are," said Kaytel. "They're just like us. They have no problem blending in."

"The Central Committee is worried," Dame Patmos insisted.

Kaytel made a vague gesture indicating general indifference or perhaps a total lack of interest in the opinions of the Party on the matter.

During the silence that followed, the ceiling lamps grew braver. They had attained a brightness that could now be evaluated in comparison to a number of candles. Nine, ten candles. They had increased their power and let it be known by projecting additional shadows in the room.

All cheerful expression had gone out of Dame Patmos's face.

"Here's what's been decided by the higher-ups," she announced. "We're going to send Breton out in order to have some boots on the ground. He's given us enough information; now he has to act. He has to go to rue Dellwo one way or another. Not just observe the street with special optical devices that cost an arm and a leg. He has to actually travel there and move among the dead. He's got to whack Monroe. As for the girls that are here among us, we've got to find them ourselves and whack them one by one as well. That's what's been decided."

"Breton will never do that," Kaytel objected.

Enough is enough!" Dame Patmos bellowed. "This might be the Party's last move before everything collapses. It has to work."

The glow falling from the ceiling grew ever brighter. Now Kaytel's face was clearly visible: exhausted, yellowish, and consumed by the certainty that everything was going downhill. Dame Patmos was equally visible, looking unctuous and content, at ease with herself, convinced the Party would win the battle this time, despite having lost all the others.

"It's by going where the dead are that we'll be able to start taking care of the problem," said Dame Patmos.

Kaytel's face showed great weariness and he made a gesture that caused his entire torso to move. He raised his arm as if calling on the distant founders of the Party to bear witness, their shadows floating on the ceiling among the cracks and bumps in the plaster.

"Even if we managed to send Breton to the dead, he wouldn't do it. Even if we gave him all the necessary equipment, he wouldn't kill Monroe."

"Do you see another way out?" asked Dame Patmos. "Because it's not with your defeatist way of talking that I'll be able to reassure the Central Committee."

Kaytel shook his head, pouting. He was thinking, no doubt reflecting on the accumulation of historical, political, and genetic failures, and his own uselessness in the final exploit of the ongoing shipwreck.

Then, he banged his fist on the desk, like someone who wants to show that a decision has been made. Yet there was nothing resolute in the sound produced. It rang out reticently. It expressed a hesitant decision, a bit frightened by itself, and limp.

"I can go myself," he murmured.

"Where? To the Central Committee? They won't receive you."

"No," said Kaytel in a voice that was weak but slightly less hesitant than his fist earlier. "To the dead."

Dame Patmos recoiled and grimaced. She gave the impression of having smelled a bad odor.

Seconds passed, five, six, maybe eight.

"What are you talking about, Kaytel?" she finally exhaled.

"I've studied shamanism in the past," Kaytel confessed. "I still know the basics. It's not that difficult to visit the dead."

"Bah," said Dame Patmos.

She allowed herself a moment to think.

Outside, the rain was making one heck of a commotion. The drops could be heard whipping against the windowpanes, the courtyard crackling, the gutters gurgling. From time to time, but not often, a silent lightning bolt broke through the darkness. The rumbles of thunder took their time following, but they wound up rolling through the office walls. The night and the storm had reached the hospital, the camp, the entire universe.

"I can't believe what you're saying," Dame Patmos finally sighed.

She'd stopped grimacing and once again wore her femme fatale face. Pudgy, but beguiling. Her eyes shone. Her head was rife with schemes and arguments. She was analyzing Kaytel's proposition, imagining the consequences. Among those, there was the possibility of success, greater than if Breton were assigned a mission that he would always hang back from accomplishing, even after strict conditioning by excellent trainers. Conversely, once there, Kaytel would not prevaricate when it came to Monroe. Even if the working conditions of the beyond were even more insane than in the psychiatric wards, he'd know what to do. He'd act, come hell or high water. After all, he was a seasoned police officer and had been a member of the Party since childhood who'd belonged to bizarre factions but who'd never betrayed the Party. If they sent him to kill Monroe, he would do it.

"You think you can go to the dead," she began. "But maybe you won't be able to come back."

"I don't give a damn," said Kaytel. "I belong there more than I do here."

17

The rain did not stop.

Kaytel had just taken his last drag. He stubbed out his cigarette in the ashtray. He wanted to express doubts about his chances of coming back victorious from the dead, but he refrained.

Dame Patmos wriggled in her chair. She emitted the warm scent of clean flesh. Her clothes smelled of closet and rain. She leaned toward Kaytel flirtatiously again, with no ambiguity.

"Before you head off to zombie land," she said, "maybe we could have a bit of fun, the two of us, no?"

"Bah," Kaytel responded.

"You and I could get back together," she suggested. "We were good together in the past. We could start over, no?"

"It wouldn't work anymore," said Kaytel. "We're passed the age of fooling around."

She winked at him theatrically and, seeing that he remained poker-faced, or at least that he had no intention of responding, she propped herself up more comfortably on her chair. She moved in such a way that provoked a friendly smile, some tenderness, even a voluptuous caress. Her vastness had something aesthetically pleasing about it, so unlike the avalanche of lumpy, dimpled flesh of the obese. In the half-light penetrated by the sounds of the downpour, reeking of the stale smell of bad tobacco, Kaytel looked at his visitor; she reminded him of a rotund and powerful animal, master of its surroundings, of its tranquility, of its desires and reflexes, a sort of communist elephant seal endowed with the face of a beautiful woman, radiant and strong-willed. He looked at her affectionately, not so much as a former lover would; more as a big or little brother. In any case, so as not to exacerbate the situation, he hid his feelings.

"Damn Dame Patmos," he said to himself—still poker-faced.

18

He took a third cigarette from his pack. It was the second to last; after this, he would have to stop smoking. He placed it between his lips. Dame Patmos lit it for him and put the matches back in her bag. She let him take two drags in silence.

"I'm going to disappear," Kaytel announced. "We'll say our farewells. I need a few days to practice my shamanism. Then I'll act without drawing attention. Even the Party mustn't know where I'll be."

"And if we need to reach you? For example, for a counter-order?"

Kaytel hesitated.

"I have a hideout," he confessed. "With a guy who's a seer or a shaman, something like that. One of my informants. He can give me some leads."

Dame Patmos whistled in surprise.

"I see," she said.

"If need be, you could leave me a message."

"Alright. Give me the address."

"I don't know if..." Kaytel began, then was silent.

"It'll stay between us, I promise," said Dame Patmos. "Even if the Central Committee grills me."

After taking a long drag from his cigarette, Kaytel expelled a cloud of smoke between them.

"What faction do you belong to at the moment?" he asked.

"Midwives of the Future," Dame Patmos admitted grudgingly.

"Fine. Give me your word as a midwife that you'll keep the secret."

"I give you my word," said Dame Patmos.

"I'll do you the kindness of believing you," whispered Kaytel. "It's on rue Tolgosane. A seedy building. Top floor."

"Number 27, by any chance?" said Dame Patmos with predatory joy.

"You know it?" Kaytel asked, surprised.

"The Party knows everything," Dame Patmos explained. "We know your informant and we know his address."

She was carnivorously content to witness Kaytel's confusion. She'd been hurt by how he'd snubbed her advances and now she could turn the tables, leaving him to understand that his sneakiness and his pathetic little secrets were childish compared to the Party's omnipotence. An omnipotence that here, in this office, she embodied.

"It's in the Baltimore sector, an area where no one ventures anymore," she continued. "We've given up trying to straighten out all the disorder."

"There's no more disorder there than anywhere else," Kaytel insisted.

"And then," Dame Patmos went on, "from what we could gather from Breton's elucubrations, rue Tolgosane is merely a few steps from the infamous rue Dellwo, isn't it? When you're there, you won't have too far to go to get to where the dead are. That's how I see things."

"Seems plausible," Kaytel agreed.

The rain was pattering in the hospital courtyard.

Every now and then, gravel would bespatter the windows, as if the crazies in the neighboring dormitory had decided to attack a police station.

One got the feeling that the conversation had been going on for hours, that it was well past midnight.

"We could turn out the lights and wait for the rain to stop," Dame Patmos suggested suddenly.

"Why?" asked Kaytel.

"We could stay here like lovers," murmured Dame Patmos with a radiant smile.

"I can't," Kaytel assured her. "Now I really have to leave."

He had no desire to go out in the deluge but, truth be told, he feared that Dame Patmos, driven by her instincts, would take advantage of the storm, the situation, and the weak lighting to remove her uniform and her undergarments and force him to face the challenge of hugging, caressing, and making love to her. No doubt he would have given in to her advances if they had found themselves in a hospital room or a motel, or if there had been a sofa in the office, but there was in fact nothing here to accommodate their lovemaking and he was horrified at the thought of a standing copulation, which would have forced him to lift her up and hold her enormous body mass against him. He'd rarely tried such an uncomfortable position, and only with partners who were lightweights, morally and especially physically. The whole exercise had seemed cumbersome to him, and he imagined that doing it again with Dame Patmos ran the risk of making it nightmarish.

He left the office, went down the corridor steeped in darkness, pushed open the door to the former clothes closet for the staff, and returned to offer Dame Patmos a yellow raincoat he'd found there.

Dame Patmos was pouting, and she accepted with a pouty mouth the coat Kaytel had gone to get for her. She was obviously lamenting not having had the time to bring the last aggressive stage of her plan to fruition.

"My darling's gallantry knows no limits," she said mockingly as she unfolded the raincoat, which gave off the stale smell of decomposing plastic matter.

Kaytel pretended not to notice the bitterness of her comment and went to unhook his own raincoat from the opposite wall. It resembled an ugly dried-out gargantuan bat.

"You coming?"

Dame Patmos pouted again.

"Don't think so," she said. "It's raining too hard. I'm going to put out the light and take a nap until it calms down."

"Fine," said Kaytel.

He put on his bat and went out.

He'd arrived at the ramp that was previously used to facilitate the arrival of stretchers and stood still in order to benefit a few moments more from the protection of the awning. He reached in a pocket for his last cigarette. As he was slipping two fingers in what remained of his pack, he let out a sigh of frustration. He'd left without asking Dame Patmos for a light. And, of course, there was no question of going back and confronting her foul mood.

Torrential noises were crushing the space around him.

The rain strafed the night. The lightbulb above the gatehouse at the entrance had at last reached its cruising light. It was reflected in a shifting, rippling black lake that stretched to both sides of the wide-open gate.

Kaytel buttoned the top button of his raincoat and slipped his head inside the transparent hood that rounded out the outfit. He'd put his unlit cigarette in his mouth but when he was hit in the face with the first volley of raindrops, he bent over and spit it out in the water. It had been dampened, the paper was unrolling, and in any case it had started to release on his tongue a taste that was really too far from what was acceptable for a tobacco replacement. For a minute, he watched how it floated, disintegrated, and drifted toward a sewer grate, jostled by the wavelets and sloshing water. Right next to the door, a drainpipe from the roof was spewing and churning the rainfall. He waited a moment longer, trying to separate the noises, those produced by this waterfall and those originating directly from the downpour.

Enough time wasted, he thought suddenly.

Rue Tolgosane, he thought again. Too bad that fat nymphomaniac knows exactly where I'm going to disappear.

He turned his head toward the police station. All the front windows were black, his as well. Dame Patmos had shut off the light and was standing at the window. She seemed to be watching and this surveillance caused him to lose any desire to wave. He lowered his head and crossed the courtyard. The rain drummed on his hood; his shoes splattered the hem of his trousers.

Now he turned his back to his former mistress and walked away, no doubt forever. "Damn Dame Patmos," he thought again but, perhaps because raindrops were trying to get under his collar, or because the idea that he was being observed rattled him, this time he thought of her without compassion.

19

Contrary to what he'd claimed an hour earlier, Kaytel had practically no knowledge of shamanism and no clue how to reach the dead to whack Monroe. He'd really proposed the idea to escape from Dame Patmos. Only Breton, in a pinch, could travel from one universe to the other, all the way to Monroe's dreams. And even if this skill belonged to what the Party called "shamanism," it was not yet possible to organize a commando mission on that basis alone. Teleportation was far from perfected, and the information Breton offered in dribs and drabs was often false about what he saw, what he knew, about his fidelity to the Party and about himself; he lied about everything. The investigation of Monroe and his girls is at a standstill, thought Kaytel. Operation Assassinate Monroe would go nowhere. From the start, Monroe and his girls had been assured of victory. No one will be able to get in their way, he thought.

Anyway. May as well try, he thought again.

With or without shamanism, whether we rely on Breton, my informant, or me, we'll hit a wall, thought Kaytel.

Borgmeister, he thought.

That was the name of his informant on rue Tolgosane. The one with the place where he'd counted on hiding to pursue his investigation, his mission, or simply to do nothing and get away from the Central Committee. But now that hope was already shipwrecked because Dame Patmos knew the exact address of the hideout where he'd hoped to be left in peace. He could either do nothing or follow his investigation to the end, but he wouldn't be able to hide.

He'd lost all contact with Borgmeister. Back when they'd been in touch, the man was practicing as a warlock, shaman, or clairvoyant. He had a limited clientele who chatted with and confided in him and, and when he'd extracted everything from them that could be useful to the police, he gave the dregs to Kaytel. In exchange, Kaytel intervened so that the veterinarian and ideological commissions would leave him in peace. When the authorities had withdrawn from the Baltimore sector, this fruitful dialogue between them had been interrupted and never started up again.

Kaytel recalled the interviews he'd done with him, in the dives on rue Tolgosane or on the deserted avenues. Borgmeister never denounced the patients who came to see him for exorcisms or other bullshit of the sort, but he composed useful syntheses on the state of the social, political, and psychiatric anarchy in which the Baltimore sector found itself. He was a valuable source. And, deep down, he was also an interesting guy, full of humor, full of mystery, capable of taking on his role of collaborator, cynical fellow traveler and, at the same time, claiming to belong to a libertarian-influenced dissident faction. On the question of the difference between the dead and the living, between the sane and the insane, and between the members of the Party and the traitors to the Party, his points of view were original, but there was nothing shocking about them: he lumped them all together.

Who knows, Kaytel started to think, if Borgmeister isn't linked to Monroe these days. Could be his type. Who knows if his clairvoyant powers are stronger than Breton's. Maybe without those glasses that cost an arm and a leg he can follow the comings and goings of the Monroe girls.

I'm going to find that Borgmeister, he repeated to himself. He's from the neighborhood, he must have heard of rue Dellwo and Monroe. Perhaps he's even run into the girls. What's the risk in following that lead? I may come across something interesting.

For myself, he thought. For my own information. Not for that fatso of the Central Committee.

20

He advanced deep into the rain and the dark.

Here he is. The image comes into focus as soon as he leaves the courtyard of the Cornelius Ward.

He advances deep into the rain and the dark.

He turns down avenue Chouïgo, crosses Dadirboukian Square and, for half an hour, walks along Vandal Sisters Avenue. He's heading toward the Baltimore sector. Mentally, he runs though the buildings and dormitories, those he can recognize or those that have retained, if not their original purpose, at least a plaque reminding one of it. Venerology. Gastroenterology. Dermatology for the Blind. Jean Freek Dormitory. Seeking Veterinarian. Hospice Care. Xenological Surgery. Society of the Friends of China. Fetal Medicine, Reproduction, and Genetics. Political Services. Technical Services. Intensive Care.

The psychiatric camp is humongous. The path seems endless. Sidewalks and roadways merge for hundreds of meters. The lighting is defective everywhere. The rain drums on Kaytel's raincoat. It falls straight down but, because the plastic hood offers poor protection, the rain drenches his face. Droplets collect along his earlobes, snake down to his neck. He thinks of the rain with hatred. Sometimes he can no longer see his feet and it feels as if he's walking on a river's surface. Mutant plane trees spurt from the asphalt and block his way, along with enormous fig trees. He zigzags in the roar of the downpour, he avoids the trees by placing his hand on them, as if the trees were hurling themselves at him, as if he had to push them back to go on. He doesn't avoid the puddles.

Encephalopathy. Police Retirement Home. Center for Burn Victims. Tropical Diseases.

He turns toward rue Tolgosane. He's never been inside Borgmeister's place; back in the day they would meet somewhere else in the Baltimore sector, but once, Kaytel had accompanied his informant, who'd had too much to drink, to the corner of his street. He remembers the house. He remembers the number on a little plaque above the door. There. Number 27.

It's a four-story house with a front lamp that's working. The light timer in the entrance is also working. Kaytel presses the button, shakes out his raincoat to drain off the extra liters of water, wipes his neck. He goes down the six meters of hallway that separate him from the stairs and starts climbing up. The stairway is wide but lacks ventilation, smelling of fermented onions, dross, and cat pee.

He's about to climb up the three flights but, on the second floor, he stops. Beneath the landing lightbulb are two dead people. The light goes out, Kaytel feels along the wall to reach the switch and turns it back on.

The dead people are sitting on the steps, one behind the other, a man and a woman dressed like moderately poor schizophrenics. Both of them are in a normal sleeping position, left shoulder and head comfortably nestled against the wall, legs parted without worrying about what perhaps when they were alive would have been called modesty, or dignity. Their arms rest on their thighs, their hands hang wherever they can. They look limp and grim.

"Borgmeister, fourth floor," says Kaytel, as if the couple were the building's concierges.

The man opens one eye. He stares at Kaytel for a second then mumbles a few syllables. Kaytel interprets them. This isn't the first time he's spoken with the dead, far from it. Over the years, he's learned to translate the murmurs and grunts that leak out of the recently deceased. He understands that the man is confirming the floor on which Borgmeister lives, under the eaves. He thanks him for the information with a wave of his hand. The dead man has closed his eye again and no longer reacts to anything.

Kaytel passes the man and woman and, when he reaches the fourth and final floor, he stops to take a breath. No matter what, you always feel ill at ease when you have to skirt around corpses to climb stairs.

The door to Borgmeister's room is not locked. It's slightly ajar.

Kaytel cocks an ear to listen for a possible presence and, since he hears nothing more than the patient nibbles of a wood-boring insect busily digging a tunnel in the floor or in a beam, he pushes the door and enters the minuscule apartment. He turns on the light switch to make sure no one is lurking in the shadows. He waits for the lamp to give off a little more light and looks around in the shower room and the bathroom. He urinates, flushes the toilet, and goes to sit in the armchair jammed between the bed and the wardrobe. The bed is made: a brownish blanket, gray sheets. The bedroom is furnished in a depressingly functional manner, without the slightest personal touch. The wardrobe contains a heavy coat of brown wool in bad shape, two shirts, a black sweatshirt inscribed with gaudy letters—"With the Diehards"—workers' overalls, an empty hanger, a pair of rubber boots. All the pockets are empty. The two drawers contain a change of underwear, a necklace made of the feathers and skulls of very tiny animals, and garlands decorated with coins. The usual paraphernalia of a small-time shaman. Leaning over, Kaytel notices a little cardboard suitcase sitting under the bed in the dust. He drags it toward him and opens it. A dark blue scarf, feather bouquets, a roll of copper wire, more underwear. Nothing unusual.

Kaytel places the suitcase back under the bed and stands up. He then sits on the edge of the bed and realizes he hasn't taken off his raincoat and he's about to get the bed wet. He stands up again. He grabs the empty hanger, goes over to the shower, and hangs up his bat. Not too many toiletries in the little bathroom. A toothbrush, a towel, a bar of soap. He goes to shut off the lamp. Then sits down again. This time the box spring squeaks briefly, then quiets. There's nothing else to find anywhere besides nail clippings, dust bunnies, maybe hairs. He's not interested. He's not carrying out a criminal investigation. He doesn't suspect Borgmeister of anti-Party activities. He simply wishes to find him, to make him speak, like in the old days, about an area where the police have proved to be powerless, about Monroe and the girls. In the event the informant would have a lead, you never know, or rather, it's almost certain he will have a lead, even several.

It's very late, the weather is horrendous, Borgmeister won't come home tonight, Kaytel could remain here to wait for him, he could also go look for a shelter somewhere in the Baltimore sector. At first he'd thought of asking Borgmeister to put him up, but now that Dame Patmos knows the address on rue Tolgosane, he thinks he should hide somewhere else. There's no lack of empty buildings, he'd have no trouble squatting a place in the area. Kaytel hesitates. He's not tempted by the thought of going outside again in the deluge. He listens to the rain sputtering on the roof, on the skylight, the water gurgling in the gutters. The atmosphere is conducive to meditation. He decides to remain motionless for another moment, sitting on the edge of the bed, thinking.

The window is held partly open by a toothed rack. The warm damp comes in from outside, along with the clamor of the rain and the weak light from the street. The muggy mist and the noises don't bother Kaytel any more than the dark does. The light timer on the landing has gone out. Around him are the stale smells of an abandoned room. In his mind, all the lines of his mission are heavy with darkness and have become tangled. To renew ties with Borgmeister, to call on his ambivalence as a former informant, to convince him to enter one last time in the service of the police, figure out with him how to reach Monroe shamanically, to reach Monroe and then, once there, at the scene, decide whether to kill him or to calmly stay with him among the dead. Bring Breton into the Baltimore sector, drag him from his routine observation of rue

Dellwo, and, once there, have him walk along the tracks of the former tramway until he finds the street in Monroe's dreams, the building from which the girls tumble from the night of the dead to gain a foothold in the night of the real world. Pummel Breton until he collaborates. But also, to be done with Dame Patmos. To be done with surveillance and the demands of the Party. And also, to be done with it all. Break it off once and for all. Break with everything.

He's hung his raincoat in the shower room to let it drip its last drops, and it seems to him that from time to time he hears a tinkling on the enamel of the tub, but the noise of water coming from outside is overwhelming and overrides the rest.

He tries to think about what Monroe is plotting, about shamanic practices about which he knows very little, and about the girls Monroe has introduced into the camp. For a minute or two, he envies Breton who has seen them, seen them be born and disappear and who, most likely, still knows much more about them than what he ends up saying when he's been roughed up. Then, this deep reflection leads Kaytel first to the question of his relations with Dame Patmos, then very soon afterward his mind wanders to the problems that have obsessed him forever: madness, death, life and illness after death, not to mention the series of disasters and bad choices that are leading humanity to its end. A stupefying accumulation of bad choices and bad luck.

The rain is pouring violently over the night.

The rain is hacking at the leaves on the trees.

The rain is making the stench of rot rise all the way to the rooftops of rue Tolgosane.

The rain is losing its intensity. Other sounds can be heard.

The bat raincoat is dripping on the tile of the shower room.

Perhaps I should get back together with Dame Patmos, Kaytel thinks. Have her come to rue Tolgosane, disappear with her in the Baltimore sector. For all I know, she might want to change her life as well. For all I know, she's depressed like me but she's hiding it. Like me.

He moves his hand to extract something to smoke from his pocket, then decides not to, then tries to find another position on the edge of the bed, remembers the two dead people waiting below, between the second and third floors.

And if I went to question them? he wonders.

I could ask them what they know, he thinks. They're Borgmeister's neighbors. Perhaps they could give me one or two useful bits of information.

In any case, it would break up the monotony of my night, he thinks.

21

The light timer shuts off just as Kaytel is reaching the second floor. He goes down a few more steps cautiously, then comes to a halt. He knows the two dead people he climbed around on the way up are still in the same place and he wants his eyes to grow accustomed to the darkness before he goes any farther. He has absolutely no desire to bump into the man or woman and no desire either to grope with the tip of his foot while advancing slowly, like a predator trying to surprise them.

A glimmer is filtering down from a skylight pierced between two floors. When the image of the staircase begins to appear dimly on his retinas, Kaytel notices that he's already near the couple, two stairs away from the man, who is separated from his wife by two stairs as well.

He moves half a meter to the side and sits down next to the man. The wooden staircase creaks beneath his feet and ass. Then, once Kaytel is settled, leaning against the iron rails that hold up the ramp, the creaking stops.

The staircase becomes calm again.

Kaytel no longer moves at all. He knows from experience that, in order to be accepted by the dead and so as not to indispose them, it's best to imitate them, remaining immobile for a moment. Until a relation can be established.

The rain is growing softer, you can hear it faintly falling on the other side of the minuscule window that overlooks a small courtyard. One flight down, a floor drain cannot swallow everything that's coming at it, and it gurgles loudly. Kaytel pictures the rusted grate, the cement floor around it, and farther away, shapeless boxes, ancient black plastic trashcans filled with dark water, unused for decades.

He listens to the sounds and analyzes the silence. In the house, all the apartments are empty. It's late. No one barges onto the stairway. The three of them are alone in the building with the tranquility of the night surrounding them.

"Hello," Kaytel says at last. "I'm looking for Borgmeister. Perhaps he has another address? I'd like to know if he comes here often and at what time."

His voice resonates then fades away in the dark.

After about fifteen seconds, the woman speaks. Impossible to say that she's not aware of Kaytel's presence. But she's not addressing him. She's speaking to the man, who must be her husband.

"What's that idiot want?" she grumbles grumpily.

"He's a detective," the man says. "A cop or a Party guy. They're looking for Borgmeister."

He has a voice that has trouble leaving his mouth; it comes out with whistling and bubbles, as if his throat were obstructed by blood.

"Borgmeister, from the fourth floor?" asks the woman.

"I don't know any other," says the man, mucous-mouthed.

"He must be dead," says the woman.

"A lot of good that does him," comments the man.

Inappropriate. His comment. It makes no sense.

They both are quiet for a long minute. They don't seem like they want to continue their dialogue.

Kaytel waits a little, then, since nothing is forthcoming, he makes up his mind.

"He left some things in his room," he says. "Feathers, amulets. Even in the drawer of his bedside table. It looks like sorcerer material."

His words don't bring forth any commentary. Kaytel waits patiently, then starts again.

"This Borgmeister. Was he the kind to deal in witchcraft?"

After some twenty seconds, the woman, again, addresses her husband.

"That idiot's still here?" she asks, with a savagery meant to wound Kaytel.

"Who?"

"The idiot cop."

"Yeah, he's sitting next to me," says the husband. "He says Borgmeister had sorcery material in his drawers."

The woman emits a sort of chortle. Maybe she finds all this a laughing matter, but most of all, she wants to prove she's not nice.

"One day someone stuffed something in *my* drawers," she said at last. "Quite unexpectedly. Do you remember?"

"Course I remember. And then you *was* expecting. But not for long."

"Even if it hadn't gone away by itself, I would've got rid it."

"Was it mine?" the husband asks in an even raspier and more bullous voice than before, and slightly anxiously, as if he were reviving a doubt that had long tormented him when he was alive and he'd finally found the perfect moment to dispel it.

"Don't know," says the woman. "You don't never know who foists that on you."

"Just asking," says the husband. "I don't give a damn."

They take a breather.

"So what does he want, the asshole cop?" asks the wife.

"He's wondering if Borgmeister was involved in witchcraft."

"He's asking *us*?"

"Seems so. He's saying words with his mouth voice. And they're aimed at us."

"That asshole knows nothing about witchcraft," the wife states.

And with that, the discussion is closed for a long moment.

The rain keeps falling, then it stops. Kaytel and the two dead people ruminate while listening to the last of the rain. The sounds have changed. You can distinctly hear the drops beading on a zinc ledge in the little courtyard. The water is flowing at a rolling boil toward the drains and it makes itself heard. All around the building, the pipes hiss and murmur. The damp reaches the stairway and awakens the stale smells of former greasy kitchens, badly cleaned toilets, and spiders.

Now that Kaytel is used to the dark, he can better make out the shapes of the two dead people. They are dressed as if on their way to a mass grave and they aren't moving. Kaytel, with his ancient raincoat and his oppressed stoop, is not so different from them.

"Okay then," Kaytel says at last, "just between us, what do you know about Borgmeister?"

No one answers for two, three minutes. Long minutes filled with the sounds of water and the odors of tegenarie, stuffed cabbage, and soiled toilet bowls.

Then the wife responds.

"Why's he bugging us, that asshole?" she says crossly. "Why don't he go interrogate Monroe if he don't know how to spend his night?"

"Shut up," hawks the husband. "Do not mention Monroe. It's like he don't exist."

"Who mentioned Monroe?" the wife says defensively. "I didn't even pronounce his name. I don't pronounce the name of someone who don't exist."

"I must've misheard," the man admits. "I thought you were talking about him."

"Yeah, yeah," says the woman. "You thought wrong. You hearing voices."

22

Kaytel's relationship with the dead couple was not good. The old man and the old woman were not in the mood. Kaytel stayed next to them for a long time without saying anything more, then stood up. He didn't really know how to continue the interview, if you could even call it an interview. He climbed up a few stairs toward the light timer button, thought for a second that the light might change something, then, without touching the button, climbed down again. The stairs creaked. He sat back down.

Once the echo of the creaking had faded, the staircase grew quiet again. The rain had stopped and from outside came only the single notes of straggler droplets.

The two dead people were very close to him. Their odor of worn-out clothing and suet rose toward him and now that his eyes were accustomed to the shadows, he could make out that they were sitting in a defensive posture, as if they thought Kaytel were going to kick them in order to dislodge them. From time to time, they coughed or hawked. They didn't change position, they didn't tremble, but nonetheless they seemed to be expecting the worst. Kaytel tried to estimate how long they'd been there. Judging from their behavior and the smells swirling around them, their deaths must not have occurred more than four or five days previously.

Four or five days, thought Kaytel. So they're still in good shape.

"Hey, you two," said Kaytel. "I don't want to harm you. I just want to talk a bit."

"About what?" said the man, without turning to face Kaytel.

"About one of the building's tenants," said Kaytel, as if the subject hadn't been broached half an hour ago.

"Borgmeister?"

"Yeah. Can you tell me what he was doing up there on the fourth floor?"

"He was doing what we all do. Waiting without stirring. Perchance he sang every now and then. One or two girls came to see him."

"Girls? What kind of girls?"

The man let out a nasal sigh, a kind of weary groan, then was silent. Kaytel waited for an answer for a long minute, then he gave up expecting one and sighed in turn.

Raindrops rang intermittently in the courtyard below, behind the skylight window. Again Kaytel envisioned the minuscule little courtyard, a sordid, pitch-dark place, a dead end where nobody ever came, a jumble of soggy boxes and scrap metal and trash bins without lids, filled to the brim with water.

Then the man broke the silence.

"Do the police still exist?" he asked with curiosity.

His throat was clogged with mucus and dust. Vibrations had trouble moving beyond his vocal cords.

"Yes," Kaytel confirmed. "There are still several of us. No unit has collapsed. The hospitals, the police, everything is still functioning normally. The Party is still there to watch over us and our future. There are no problems anywhere. It's just that there are fewer and fewer of us."

"I have no mind to collaborate with the police," the man declared.

The conversation stood at a standstill again. Behind the skylight a bleak, diffuse light did nothing to attenuate the dark. Several minutes passed.

Suddenly, the woman, whose mouth had remained shut until then, asked, "What does that bozo want?"

"It's a cop bastard," said the man. "He wants us to collaborate with him."

"About what?"

"About the dead and the girls who went up to see Borgmeister and never came back down."

"Maybe it's about time the police took care of that," growled the woman.

"Well, let them take care of it without me," the man bristled. "Me, I've already said I'm not about to cooperate."

"Well, I'm of two minds," said the woman. "They sometimes do good work and it's not always easy for them. We could actually give them a hand."

"You always have been on the side of the authorities," scolded the man.

"And you've always been a non-Party," remarked the woman. "You can't understand. Being faithful to our first ideals. You can't understand."

"This fuckwit said everything was still functioning normally," the man coughed out. "And that the Party had not collapsed."

"Course it hasn't collapsed," said the woman proudly. "It'll last till the bitter end. We'll all be dead and buried to a man and the Party will still be there."

"And what purpose will it serve, your Party," the man argued, "if no one's left?"

"It'll watch over us and our future," said the woman proudly.

III

23

Breton had just suggested I leave the window and that we return to our chess match. I was about to move when, at the spot where the roof of the house we were watching had been slashed, a hand appeared, followed by an arm. Then the first half of the body of the girl. She began by carefully groping around to gauge the resistance of the edges of the opening. It had been caused by a partial collapse of the framework, and it also resembled a hole made by a missile. In any event, the girl was exploring the tears. Above her, slates were coming off fluidly, six, seven, perhaps eight, and they slid off slowly before plunging into the void. The girl let them drop, then managed to extract herself from the eaves and climb over the gutter, obviously with the help of a rope she had attached to a sturdy beam. From this distance, the rope was invisible, but she could not have reached the façade solely by means of her sense of balance and her grip. She was carrying communications equipment, a heavy, antediluvian radio, bags, and a small rifle the barrel of which barely extended beyond her shoulder. She crossed the level of the gutter, descended three meters along the wall at lightning speed, then stopped dead between the fourth and third floors. She must have been caught on a cement or stone relief.

Stuck between the fourth and third floors.

The rain was falling in wide vertical sheets and it blurred the image. It also blurred the sound. It was impossible to know if the girl was screaming, if she was calling for help, or if she remained silent. The water streamed torrentially in the shadows, along the dark, vertical, mildly decrepit walls, onto the flooded sidewalk, along the slats in the blinds, on the darkened windows of all the houses in the street. Farther away there were plane trees with branches raised, indifferent to the deluge. No tram tracks, no cables weaving a bizarre network above the ground. It was not rue Dellwo. The girl remained motionless, neither trying to climb back up nor slide farther down, as though she had given up on everything. At present she was wrapped in a cloak that gave her a spherical shape, extremely disagreeable to look at because it was difficult to discern a human form there.

Next to me, Breton fidgeted. On his nose he wore bulging eyeglasses and, to prevent his breath from fogging them up, he wore a surgical mask that hid the bottom of his face. The top of his shirt was weighed down by the magic scrap metal, the cowbell necklace, and the leather amulets that we had decided a week ago to add to our observers' panoply. It had been my idea. I tended to think that openly shamanic material could not harm our undertaking, in which a portion of oneirism and magic was already at work, if only in the Hirsch glasses, which were far from using solely optical means.

Between sky and earth, the girl was making tiny movements under her tarp.

"She wants to establish communication," Breton declared in a strained voice.

"She hasn't touched her radio equipment," I objected.

Breton began to wobble next to me. He steadied himself on my shoulder and moved away. He was breathing chaotically, no longer gazing at what we'd been examining since nightfall. He removed his surgical mask and placed it hurriedly on the chessboard amid the pieces, some of which fell and rolled on the floor: a black bishop, the white queen, two pawns. Then he leaned against the wall, slumped down and, a few seconds later, was squatting on the floor. A yellowish trickle slid from his half-open mouth.

“She’s attempting a telepathic call,” he whispered.

He’d continued to hold the semi-spherical lenses of the Hirsch glasses in front of his eyes. I glanced one last time toward the street. I don’t know the camp well enough to identify or name with any certainty all the nooks and crannies, but it seemed to me that the spot was real, a little street situated in the Baltimore sector. It was not rue Dellwo. It was real and, despite my poor memory, I think I’d already wandered around there at least two or three times over the last decades. But perhaps I was wrong. The night was frighteningly dark, the downpour had doubled in intensity, it was hard to make out any details.

The girl was still hanging onto a relief in the façade, then she dropped. Now she was out of sight.

Breton had ended up sitting on the floor. He refrained from groaning. Sweat and tears were dripping on the metal parts of his enormous glasses. A yellow liquid was escaping between his lips, dribbling onto his chin. Receiving a message telepathically causes excruciating pain, or a discomfort so incapacitating that it can be mistaken for pain. Anyone who has experienced this knows what I’m talking about. The military doctors know too, which explains why their guinea pigs for oneiric voyages are not soldiers but simply subhumans and freaks.

“I’ve got the communication,” Breton murmured.

“Relax,” I said.

Breton stretched out his arms for an instant, as if he were seeking support in the void. Then he clenched his ankles with his hands.

“She’s speaking in short sentences,” he said. “I hear her name. She’s exhausted. Her name is Lola. Lola Schnittke.”

“Are you sure?” I asked.

“Yes,” said Breton. “Schnittke. She’s whispering her name again. She just fell to us. She thinks she’s already dead. She thinks she’s leaving the world of the dead to enter into our free-floating world.”

Breton’s teeth were chattering. Strong jolts of electricity were coursing through him.

Afraid of forgetting the girl's name, I went to spit on the condensation on the window and immediately wrote it as best I could with the nail of my right index finger. Then I went back to Breton. His glasses, much more impressive than aviator glasses, made him look like a blind foot soldier fighting the abominations of the world. All the shamanic gris-gris, the cowbells, and the tufts of magic fur he had pinned to his hospital jacket shivered along with him.

I placed a hand on his shoulder. Through the fabric, I could feel that his flesh was on fire.

"I still hear her," he said. "I think she's dead. She's maintaining contact. She's speaking from her death. She doesn't know she's already entered our free-floating world."

"What's she saying?" I asked.

"Nothing," panted Breton. "She's content just to talk."

24

I turned on the bedroom light. The bulb gave off a timid oatmeal-colored light and then, barely two minutes later, it reached full steam and began its losing battle against the semi-darkness. The bedroom appeared to be in disorder, the mattress had been moved and was now buried under our oneiro-optical equipment and bits of animal skins we rarely used—only in the event a trance necessary for our observation hadn't come for several nights in a row. The atmosphere was one of discomfort and filth. The chessboard was balanced on a red plastic stool. I was white. Stupidly, I had just castled and there was no longer any hope for my king.

Without reaching the end of the game, without waiting for the inevitable checkmate, I gathered the pieces and stuffed them pell-mell into our sports bag, along with the least bulky optical instruments and my woolens—a sweater and a scarf—in case the weather were to lose its endless warmth.

We'd decided to flee.

We knew too much and, because we had lied about almost everything, we feared the moment when Kaytel and his gang would use drastic measures to make us confess, to force us to give up the girls' names and their hiding places along with their plans of rebellion and subversion. Once that gang made up their minds, we would find ourselves recycled to the Veterinary Research Labs, facing the torturers who would make us long for our usual minions who, deep down, were not very brutal, hitting us with moderation or often just pretending.

Breton was breathing loudly. His breath had become regular once again, but he remained prostrate under the window. The telepathic contact had exhausted him. I couldn't sense his gaze behind the monstrous lenses of his glasses, but I suppose he'd closed his eyes while he waited for his organism to regain some strength.

I took advantage to erase the name I'd written in the condensation on the window. I did this regularly, inscribing the name of the girls who appeared during the black nights, the girls Monroe was sending in the hopes they'd destroy everything and put an end to the Party's hideous degeneration. The first had been Rebecca Rausch, the love of my life. More had followed. Lilia Adouldjamani. Viola Mourmansk. Mariana Magadane. Cora Kliff. Mirka Goldenberg. The last, for the moment, had been Lola Schnittke. The entire list was there, invisible after having been erased from the condensation with a rag.

"Even if you erase it, the police will be able to see it," Breton said between two breaths. "They have special powders and magnifying glasses. Nothing escapes them. Break the window."

The chessboard, I suddenly realized. I'd forgotten to put it in the bag. It was still atop the stool. The perfect tool for smashing the window to make its pieces fall into the courtyard.

The sound of breaking glass in the bedroom silence—the scraping and the small but relentless efforts to scatter the last shards out the window. Then I shook the chessboard to get rid of the sparkly dust that still stuck to it and added it to our fugitives' things.

"Good job," affirmed Breton.

I opened the door. The hallway, empty, was plunged in shadow. There were nights when our guards defected, perhaps because they found monitoring us tedious, or perhaps some private business—love affairs or mafia business—took priority. Here, their work consisted of dozing in front of the door in two broken down armchairs they'd borrowed from a nearby conference room. The odor of these chairs drifted up to my nose. They smelled of piss and sweat. I moved away from the door. Then I went to vomit in the toilet area.

Breton managed to stand up. He took my place above the toilet bowl. We each drank a little water, then Breton vomited again. As soon as he'd flushed the toilet, he declared himself ready.

I turned off the lamp, hoisted my bag on my shoulder, and slammed the door behind us. The House of Cosmonauts echoed with the sound, then silence returned. Still suffering from the telepathic contact, Breton walked with difficulty. I offered him my arm so he could climb down the stairs without losing his balance.

Once on the street, Breton went to hug a plane tree and began to whisper his secrets to it. It must have been three in the morning. There was no sign of life in the neighboring buildings. The air was damp, the temperature pleasant. I placed the bag on the ground and lit a cigarette while waiting for Breton to finish with the plant world.

I was close enough to him to hear that he wasn't confiding any secrets about the inquiry, nothing in relation to the girl who had left her world of the dead to join us. No, he was speaking to the plane tree like it was a dear friend, talking to it about himself. He said he had vomited, that the light from the bedroom lamp was feeble, that I'd made noise when I broke the window, and that, if we hadn't had to interrupt our game, he would have had me in checkmate in two moves. He expressed his compassion for the tree and apologized for not being able to remove it immediately from its miserable stretch of tar in order to replant it somewhere else, among its kind, in a forest where no human or humanoid brute would ever set foot. He tried to put himself in the tree's place and asked it to continue to be patient. He promised that it would soon see the camp rid of the last of its patients and the last of its alleged "well people" and then, with its kind, the tree would be able to find peace.

His prayer finished, he urinated like a dog against the trunk, then signaled to me.

The night was almost warm. It wasn't raining. We were alone.

I hoisted the bag again, swearing to myself at the excessive weight of our equipment. We walked down boulevard Badbachdaf and, after strolling for almost two hours along the hospital buildings, neighborhoods, and dormitories, we met up with avenue Chouïgo. Soon we reached the courtyard of the Waldemar Ward. We had left it weeks ago. In a way, we'd returned to our starting point in this story.

Breton was stumbling from exhaustion. He could no longer keep up with me. I turned toward him. He could hardly stand; he was livid and trembling.

"I can't go on," he confessed.

I put down the sports bag. I'd thought he'd recuperated from his earlier trance and I'd let go of his arm for the last kilometer. In reality, he was in a pitiful state.

"The girl keeps calling," he whispered.

"Tell her not to trust anything," I said.

Breton had trouble breathing.

"Lola . . ." he panted. "Watch out . . . Don't trust anything. I'm coming to you. Remember the meeting place. Be careful . . ."

He was sitting against a plane tree. He'd let himself slide to the ground. He spoke no more.

We stayed like that for five or ten minutes, in the dark, in the quiet.

"We could go into the ward," I said. "That's where we were before the House of Cosmonauts. We had a room there. We could settle back in there."

"No," said Breton. "We decided to get out of this place. They'll be able to find us again if we stay. They mustn't."

"Okay," I said. "Let's keep moving."

I looked at the portion of avenue Chouïgo that could be seen from the courtyard. Plane trees, lindens, the failing light of the streetlamps, and the sidewalk, damp from the last shower. A group of four schizophrenics meandered beneath the trees.

"There's no one in the streets," I commented.

"There's no one anywhere," said Breton.

25

Kaytel had gone to get his raincoat on the fourth floor; he'd decided to go out to get some fresh air rather than hang around with the dead for no reason. The light timer went out when once again he neared the second floor. He let his retinas perceive anew a few images of black on black, then continued on his way. The dead were still there. He skirted the man and woman.

"And here's that jerk again, dripping on us with his coat that stinks of a wet rag," complained the woman.

"Bah, it's just a few drops," said the man, toning things down.

"It's flowing toward me," said the woman. "It's going to wet my bottom."

From the couple wafted the odors of grimy cupboards. No one had bothered to wash those two or block their orifices before they'd decided to rise from the dead and they were wearing clothes that should have gone straight into a dirty laundry basket. Kaytel was not particularly sensitive to the smell, so he continued down the stairs without holding his breath. When he reached the bottom, however, he stopped to gather his wits about him, as if the stench had made him dizzy.

He'd reached the ground floor. The door to the street stood ajar. He pulled it toward him and crossed the threshold. Immediately he was surrounded by nocturnal darkness and beset by the rain that had just begun again. It fell vertically, powerfully, and it had already begun hammering at his head and shoulders. He pulled on the hood of his raincoat and started striding forward on the sidewalk. He left rue Tolgosane on his right and went into a small street, then came to an avenue he didn't recognize.

He'd barely gone a hundred meters when someone came loose from a façade and fell in front of him like a dark mass. Water from a puddle splattered his face, a layer atop the raindrops. Reflexively he drew back a few steps, wiping his eyes, then approached the hunched shape on the damp ground. It was a girl dressed like a commando, weighed down by military gear composed of several bags, a weapon resembling a lead pipe, and a massive radio protected by a Bakelite flap.

The girl shook herself, put her joints back in place, and gathered her gear together slowly, as if Kaytel weren't two meters from her. She was still sprawled in a puddle and, now that she had moved, her back was to Kaytel.

"Fuck!" she grumbled. "I could have left some of it behind!"

The rain streamed over her, on the bonnet that hid her head and hair, on her upper body so encumbered with pouches and bags that Kaytel couldn't manage to see whether she was normally built or deformed. He wondered about it because her appearance, in the night and the dark water, had something strange about it. She didn't seem to have suffered from the fall. She must be trained for that, Kaytel thought. She must be one of Monroe's girls. She has military training. She was taught to jump from windows; she's used to plummeting along walls without a rope to catch her. She remained a little stunned on the sidewalk for a few seconds, but she's already recovered. Now she's swearing like a sailor and moving around as if she hadn't just dropped several meters. She's sturdy, this girl.

Still, I can't see what she looks like, he thought. What if it isn't really a girl?

Being careful to stay beyond her reach, in case she's aggressive, he went to stand in front of her to look at her. He couldn't make out anything decisive. The nearby trees reduced the light from the street even more. The girl's face, barely discernable, seemed stubborn, gloomy, not kind. Her body disappeared in the shadows and it was almost impossible to know if, under all the clothes and bags, an athlete or a skinny adolescent was hidden.

The girl remained lumped in the puddle, indifferent to Kaytel and the rain, and she was leaning over her radio as if trying to shroud it to keep out the water. Then she turned a few knobs. The internal lamp began to glow, not enough to light up the entire device or the girl's stomach and hands. A scrambled noise could be heard, coughing and sputtering. The girl turned a knob and the crackling diminished, replaced by a man's voice, terribly distant, terribly tired and wavering.

That voice is familiar, thought Kaytel.

"Lola . . . Don't lose contact . . . Your sisters will join you . . . Hide . . . Now . . . You are . . . You are no longer . . ."

Breton's voice, thought Kaytel.

Breton's voice! he thought.

"I'm coming to meet you. Beware. Don't trust anything . . ." the voice continued.

Then the communication was cut off.

"Bastards! Shitheads!" said the girl under her breath.

Kaytel took a step and bent down toward her to see her better, meet her gaze, and establish contact, a first intelligence. The girl did not raise her eyes toward him and the radio was again dark and silent. Kaytel then did something he regretted afterward but that at the time had seemed appropriate. He held his hand out to the girl to help her stand up. The girl misunderstood his gesture, got to her feet, and jumped back, making a fierce splash in the puddle where until then she had been squatting calmly. Once again Kaytel was struck in the face with a burst of muddy water. He protested. Ten meters from him, the girl was now standing under a tree, bent over what Kaytel believed was a metal truncheon but that was in reality a sawed-off shotgun. In the blink of an eye she'd had time to gather up the radio and her gear, spatter Kaytel to neutralize or delay him, take a spectacular leap, and aim the black tube of her weapon at him.

"Hey, you there!" cried Kaytel. "What the . . ."

The girl seemed faceless and shapeless with, in the shadows, that iron mouth that obviously wanted to spit its fire on Kaytel's raincoat and, fairly shapeless as well, on Kaytel himself.

"Don't shoot!" he exclaimed in an exhausted voice.

Two seconds went by. The rain beat down on the hood of his raincoat and also, because tension made him sensitive to everything—to movement, to noise—he distinctly heard the racket the raindrops were making all around him, on the sidewalk, on the branches of the plane tree near which the girl had landed after her acrobatic leap.

"I don't want anything, I don't even want to know who you are," Kaytel lied so that the silence between them didn't slide into uncontrollable violence.

The girl didn't move a millimeter.

"I'm from the Party," Kaytel offered. "It's been forty years since anyone has shot at us. That's in the past. Calm down, will you. Is—"

The girl shot. Kaytel felt the projectile hit him and he shook his head in a gesture that was a mixture of incredulity and disappointment. Then he felt pain in the middle of his ribcage and took a step or two back. Without really knowing why, he raised an arm, threw off his hood, and began spinning slowly next to a puddle of very dark water. He was attentive to the sounds of the rain as if it weren't falling on him and he spent several seconds in mental confusion, trying to remember exactly the number of ribs that protected the top of his torso, swaying in the water and stumbling above it. He didn't even try to gain a foothold. He wasn't looking at the girl and, when he again tried to focus on her, she had disappeared.

She'd gone toward a shadowy patch between two houses, a narrow alley perhaps, a gully of some kind, in any case a shadowy patch even darker than all the rest. She had disappeared.

Kaytel wondered if he should follow her, then let out a long, a very long sigh. It was his last.

26

With the rain drenching his face and streaming under his shirt collar, Kaytel muttered a phrase of displeasure. He was sitting on the sidewalk, in the water; the entire upper part of his body ached and he was coming out of an indeterminate period of unconsciousness.

"What the..." he protested.

He was protesting his situation, his passivity, the rain, and the whole world in general.

"What the..." he repeated.

The constant hammering of the rain echoed around him. Fifty meters ahead, the bulb of a streetlamp was fighting heroically against the gloom, the flood, and the additional shadows of the tree branches. Here and there the light exposed splotched asphalt.

He stood up and went to lean against the closest wall. He wasn't dizzy in the least. The pain stretched from his abdomen to his left shoulder, like a sling, but it was bearable. His legs were slightly unsteady. A weariness swept over him, both physical and mental. He'd already imagined, for example, letting himself slide down the wall in the rain to return to his interrupted slumber. And once again he mumbled the mere beginnings of sentences, rough sketches of thoughts colored by disgust and muddled recrimination.

Then something encouraged him to change his mood. A puff of dignity, perhaps, or the dregs of a survival instinct. He pulled away from his support, shoved his hands in his raincoat pockets, and decided not to pay much attention to the cold rain coursing along his back and stomach. Now he advanced in a street the name of which he didn't know—rue Zinkorine. He walked, swaying like a drunk, stumbling every five or six steps, but caught himself and did not fall. He turned at the first intersection. Now he was walking boldly under the rain. His steps were less tentative, the memory of places was coming back to him. He was walking in the direction opposite the one that had led him to the girl. Now he'd found rue Tolgosane again. Without needing to think, he went directly toward the entrance of the building the number of which he recalled. 27.

It's here, he thought. For the moment, it's here.

He pushed open the front door, removed his raincoat, and spent a long while shaking it out and patting his neck dry.

Worthless thing, he grumbled to himself. Lets the water in through all the holes.

The walk hadn't exhausted him; quite the contrary. It had revived him slightly and, even if he didn't feel great, he could stay upright. The pain in his chest that had overwhelmed him when he'd woken up now seemed distant. Like a ghost. It was still there, but he could forget it.

He put his raincoat back on because he had nothing in reach from which to hang it and because he wanted his hands to be free, an old cop reflex of which he wasn't even aware. He groped for a light switch. The hallway lit up and now there were two directions possible: toward the door that led to the rain-lashed little courtyard or toward the stairway. He thought it would be best to go up to the fourth floor where he knew was a place he could collapse while waiting for something better. Nevertheless, he hesitated a moment before advancing. He swayed lazily from one foot to the other. The light timer went out. He pushed it again and headed to the stairway.

On the second floor, sitting on the steps, the two dead folk were still on the job—man and woman, motionless, with eyes closed. He drew near without any particular desire to sit next to them and start a conversation, but the woman nodded and spoke.

"Look," she said. "Borgmeister's back."

"He's drenched; he's going to drip all over us," the man said.

"He probably went to see a girl," the woman suggested.

"He's at that age," said the man.

Kaytel went around them slowly. It didn't bother him to be taken for Borgmeister.

"The asshole sprayed me," the woman complained.

Her comment annoyed Kaytel.

"I'm being careful," said Kaytel defensively. "I'm taking the utmost precautions not to get anyone wet."

He stopped to point out that his raincoat had brushed against the banister, not the occupants of the stairway.

"He says he's being careful," remarked the woman.

"So, you see?" said the man, who seemed less cantankerous than his companion.

"Forgive me if I sprinkled you a bit," said Kaytel.

He paused, making sure any possible drips or drops that came off him were directed away from his interlocutors. Suddenly he felt the need to exchange a few words with them, at least to obtain proof of his continued existence, whether as Kaytel, Borgmeister, or any other individual endowed with a semblance of life or speech.

Several moments elapsed in the silence of the stairway and the roar of the rain rampaging outside.

The timer went out. Kaytel had located the switch when the light was lit. He took a few steps, pressed it, and returned with his dripping raincoat next to the dead people.

"I've had just about enough of him going and coming," growled the woman. "It's nighttime. Neighbors should shut themselves in their own places and stay there."

The curiosity of a detective flashed through Kaytel's mind. It disappeared almost immediately and, by the time he'd asked the question, he barely remembered why he'd spoken.

"Did anyone come by tonight?" he asked.

"He asked if anyone came by," said the woman. "What do we tell him?"

"Nothing," the man snarled.

"A girl?" asked Kaytel.

To tell the truth, he no longer knew exactly why he was carrying out this interrogation, nor of what girl he could be speaking. His mind was much too fuzzy.

"He's asking us 'bout the girls who come down from his place," said the woman. "The girls who come down and the girls who go up."

"More likely he wants to know if the police are on his tail," said the man.

"What's the point in knowing that?" asked the woman.

Kaytel shook his head. He didn't understand where this dialogue was going, if you could even call it a dialogue. He had no desire to pursue his inquiry. Now, more than anything, he wanted to sleep.

"We'll tell him nothing," the woman advised.

"Right. Nothing," the man agreed.

"He should go up to the fourth floor and go to bed, the twerp," concluded the woman.

Then all that remained was the sound of Kaytel's footsteps on the stairs, and the roar of the rain in the courtyard, in the street, on the roof, on the hospital, on the buildings of the psychiatric camp, on the entire city.

27

Lola Schnittke slipped between two deserted buildings, into a back alley barely a meter wide. The rain cascaded along the walls and fat drops plashed around her. The place smelled of wet cement and dereliction.

Her radio hissed weakly but not the slightest recognizable voice could be discerned behind the continual whistling.

She'd been told that, once she'd set foot in the land of the living, the radio would work both as receiver and transmitter. She'd been assured that for the first few hours she would be able to use it. Monroe or Breton would be on the other end. Then the batteries, non-rechargeable, would die and she'd destroy it as instructed.

She positioned her ear near the speaker and, after listening in vain for a minute, she flipped a hot ebonite switch to change the method of communication.

"Monroe?" she asked in a quiet voice.

She pressed the same switch to wait for the answer.

Slight crackling. A pop. No answer.

Again she flipped the switch. The machine sputtered then went silent.

"Breton?" she whispered.

The rain punctuated her waiting. No wind gusts, only an intense, regular torrent.

She waited another ten minutes. No answer.

"Fucking bastards!" she swore, opening her mouth a millimeter.

She turned off the radio.

She was in the darkness of night, in the darkness of the city battered by rain, in the darkness of an extremely narrow canyon. Still, it was nothing like the black space from which she'd come. She could see everything very clearly.

The dirty walls, the hiding places of minuscule spiders that the water hadn't managed to drown, the streaks that zigzagged across the walls and, on the ground, muddy tracks, cracks, puddles and, farther away, a few fatigued ferns.

"I'll leave it here then, this crappy thingamabob."

She was talking about the radio. Monroe had insisted it be included in the equipment. She'd never liked it. Heavy, cumbersome, almost always half-comatose. According to Monroe, it was capable of replacing telepathic communication.

"Telepathic communication my ass!" she exclaimed under her breath.

Then she squatted and stiffened. She thought she'd stay like that until dawn. She'd been trained to stay immobile for months, years even. A few hours of nocturnal catatonia wouldn't be a problem.

No one was out in the streets. The guy she'd shot a while ago had been an exception.

In the building across from her, on the other side of the avenue, no lamp was lit. In her mind she had a map and some pictures she'd studied during her gestation period, but she didn't recognize anything here. She'd been advised to go as soon as possible to a psychiatric ward. Blending into the camp and with the ward patients was to constitute the first phase of her mission. She would wait for sunrise and go look for it. Normally, it shouldn't be too hard for her to find.

"Shitty mission," she grumbled.

Then said no more.

When the night grew pale, she rose from her squat and, even though she wasn't at all stiff, she began to do some fifty bends and stretches. Her clothing crackled more than her joints. Then she peeked out of her hiding place.

The rain had stopped. The psychiatric camp was draped in a gray gloom that revived the dull colors of the walls. The avenue was a straight line, so you could see far into the distance. She scrutinized that distance, looking for human shapes. Only vegetation occupied the sidewalks, dense trees evenly spaced that were often called plane trees, mistaken for plane trees, whereas they belonged to some mutant species with evergreen leaves and black trunks.

No human shapes.

"Fuck!" Lola Schnittke swore. "It truly is a city of the dead."

Neither doctors nor patients in sight, assuming a clear distinction between the two categories existed.

"Fuck!" she swore again.

The cursing was a shortcoming that Monroe had not fought against and, in any case, he couldn't have changed it. The girls whom he'd groomed for years during exhausting specialized training, his girls, were formidable, beautiful, tough, brave, intelligent, but they were foul-mouthed. They had retained the violent, often barbaric and vulgar language of the dead. They swore like sailors from the black space. For Monroe, they were the last egalitarian warriors and their way of expressing themselves was of no importance. He had made them leave the shadows acrobatically after they'd died in order to land in the psychiatric camp; they were the armed faction of the future Party for whom he'd hoped and prayed since his execution. Never mind if their language was crude and laced with profanity.

All of a sudden she began to think back to the guy she was forced to shoot. A guy who had run toward her, to touch her, speak to her, arrest her, or who knows what.

"He was about to infect me with his germs, that fuckface," she grumbled.

In the dark recess from which she still had not emerged, she bent over the useless radio and took it apart. One or two minutes later, she tossed the pieces of wood, ebonite, Bakelite, copper, brass, aluminum, glass behind her—all very valuable materials in the place she'd come from, but totally worthless here.

"I wasn't about to burden myself with that junk!" she murmured, tossing the last crumbs of the radio beyond the first ferns.

At present, she was standing under a plane tree. To her left and right, the avenue was empty, swept by the damp and the vague glimmers of first light.

Her mission was beginning. After the two or three hours she'd needed to get used to the conditions of the living, she felt in tip-top shape. She'd been told to get on the radio during the first minutes of her arrival, to signal to Monroe that she had passed to the other side and to inform the other girls already in the sector, or Breton. And this morning, since no one had come to greet or guide her, she'd have to fend for herself. Which didn't really bother her. She'd been trained for that for years.

"Enough time wasted, goddammit!" she growled.

She didn't know where she was. Her first job was to figure that out. She went through the list of places where she was told she could have landed. Baltimore Crossroad, avenue Molinari, avenue Mong, rue Zinkorine, rue Tolgosane, boulevard Dafodilian.

"Tolgosane! Dafodilian! Stupid names!" she protested under her breath.

IV

28

Kaytel had settled into rue Tolgosane and hadn't budged.

Three days and three nights had gone by and he'd remained apathetically under the eaves in Borgmeister's crummy apartment. He didn't even wonder why he was there. Obviously, when night fell and darkness flooded the room, he could again see the nocturnal scene during which a hysterical creature had fired at him. A vague, somber sequence that he had difficulty taking for his own experience, that he couldn't manage to date, consigning it instead to distant memory, as if he were trying with difficulty to remember images from an old movie. At times he thought of the devastating pain he'd felt, thought he'd managed to get away from something and then, a moment later, he wondered idly exactly what he'd got away from. Unable to find a clear answer, he turned his attention to something else, a creaking in the roof, a belch in a pipe, a black stain on the gray rectangle of the skylight.

He sat down on the bed. Sat, not lay. And in spite of everything, his brain didn't stop working. He pondered the complications of living, surviving, and dying, for him and everyone else. From the apartment of the dead couple on the second floor, where he remembered having poked around the first day, motivated by an inexplicable policing eagerness, he'd taken a jar of pickles and a propaganda pamphlet. He hadn't yet touched the pickles. However, from time to time he'd cast a glance at the pamphlet—a publication of the "Posadists of the Ninth Month" who claimed that, after the earthly reign of the ants, man would rise from his ashes and reestablish primitive communism. He read and reread this text and, although it was slightly dissident and obsolete, he mostly agreed with it.

Occasionally his ruminations were interrupted by a cloud of somnolence in which he could not get completely lost because the rumblings and grumblings that came out of his mouth and stomach were so like injunctions from another world that they prevented him from totally losing consciousness. His shredded ribcage intruded on him regularly, but without making him suffer. The pain could even become imperceptible for hours. He refrained from exploring the wound with his fingertips and didn't examine it in the shower-room mirror. It was a fatal wound, no question about it; there was no point in musing on it further. He'd decided not to make a fuss about it and to let fate take care of it. He preferred not to spoil the future with complaints about muscle tears, tissue inflammation, ruptured heart, and other petty bourgeois bunkum.

For the sake of cleanliness, he'd removed his mud- and blood-spattered clothing and replaced them with garb from Borgmeister's drawers and closet. The shaman and he were the same size. He was slightly embarrassed to have appropriated someone else's things, but he liked the sweatshirt with "I'm with the Hardliners" written on it, and didn't regret having adopted it.

Three days, three nights. As another dreary morning dawned, he got up and, almost without thinking, slipped into Borgmeister's shamanic coat. He walked down the stairs until he reached his neighbors' second-floor apartment and entered it again. Even if the memory of it seemed interspersed with fainting spells, he recalled having made a first foray there. It had been night, he'd been hit by a bullet, he was vacillating between life and death, seeking a shelter to rest and reflect and, at the same time, he was overcome by an instinct that pushed him to nose around, rummage, and to know more about the dead couple on the stairway. He had no reason to investigate them, but he snooped. It was in his nature; in fact, it had been second nature since he'd entered the police force. He had inspected the lodging sloppily and, from the point of view of a criminal investigation, his first visit had been a fiasco. At most he'd put his hands on a jar of pickles and a little propaganda pamphlet. He'd carried them up to Borgmeister's apartment. A pathetic haul. Marinated cucurbits and an anti-Party pamphlet. He attempted to recreate his movements, his thoughts when he'd climbed over the dead to reach the fourth floor. He could remember nothing. He didn't even know if he'd spoken to them to justify the house search he'd carried out.

And, this morning, he wanted to see if there was anything else to retrieve there. It wasn't an impulse to pillage or plunder, simply the remains of his lawman curiosity, the need inscribed in his DNA to meddle in the more or less hidden lives of others.

He walked around the couple still sitting in silence on the stairs and, without a word to them, entered their apartment. In the kitchen he grabbed a second jar of Malossol pickles and a fork. There were other canned goods, metal tins, but he couldn't find a can opener so he left them. On a pile of plates a bowl rested, half filled with powdered sugar. He had no interest in that either, afraid of soiling his clothes. In any event, he had no intention of eating in the near future. It was just in case anyone came to visit Borgmeister upstairs, he thought. To offer them something before interrogating them. Next, he moved on to the living room, then the bedroom, exploring them haphazardly. The old couple didn't own anything. On a dusty shelf he picked up another "Posadists of the Ninth Month" pamphlet, identical to the one he'd been studying for three days and put it back in place. In the bedroom, the window had been opened by a gust of wind, the rain had rushed in and soaked the floorboards and a bedside rug. He took a couple of steps and beneath his soles the floor emitted the swish of a swamp. Before closing the window, he looked outside. The rain had started up again. In the dusky light, all that could be seen were black wells and the blind wet wall of the neighboring building.

Just as he was locking the espagnolette, he heard someone enter the building, go down the hallway, and begin to lumber up the stairs that led to the second floor. So as not to be caught like a perpetrator pilfering from a stranger's home, he hurriedly left the old couple's apartment and found himself face to face with the newcomer on the landing. Face to face, and despite the half-light, he recognized him. It was Strummheim, one of the cops who'd previously obeyed his orders. One of the minions in charge of guarding and beating Breton. The man was breathing with difficulty; climbing the stairs seemed to have exhausted him and he was wheezing convulsively, a ludicrous accordion note escaping at the end of each exhale. He'd grown older, his features drooped.

Kaytel immediately thought that he must be dead, too. Fucking shit, he thought, adopting the flowery language of the newly deceased. That yokel bit the dust, too? Shit, we all croaked or what?

"Strummheim," he called in the voice of an officer addressing a soldier, "what the hell are you doing here?"

The minion raised his head and hesitated a handful of seconds while reflecting noisily. His gaze wavered. He didn't recognize his boss. Perhaps because the lighting was poor, perhaps because Kaytel was wearing clothing that changed his appearance—a shaman's outfit and an ideologically suspect sweatshirt calling on you to fight on the side of the hardliners. Perhaps also because, like Kaytel, he had just gone through the ordeal of pain and death, and on coming out the other side had gaps in his memory. Regardless, the fact was, he didn't recognize Kaytel.

"How do you know my name, Borgmeister?" he asked at last.

Kaytel shrugged. He was holding the jar of pickles in front of him and wasn't proud to expose the product of his plundering in this way. Perhaps the other man's eyesight was blurry from strain, breathlessness, and the first difficult hours of death.

In any case, Strummheim made no comment about the petty theft and climbed a few more stairs to sit next to the old man and woman who were passively watching the meeting. Kaytel did the same. There were now four of them in the semi-darkness of the stairway, united in something that resembled profound exhaustion. The old couple's eyes were closed, the two cops' were barely open. They seemed to have come together to enjoy a show in front of them, a movie for example, that was slow to materialize. In truth, everything was very dark and nothing was happening. Four dazed spectators turned toward the void.

The sound of the rain filled the space. In the stock-still semi-darkness, it was the only manifestation of the universe's existence.

"I never imagined that Borgmeister was a thief," the old man said suddenly, loudly enough to compete with the outside din, the crackling, the frenzied drumming.

With that, the conversation took off immediately, as if it had only been waiting for this first signal to flourish after having been held back, held back for too long.

As usual, the old woman defended the Party.

"He's with the Posadists of the Ninth Day," she objected. "You've got to give him the benefit of the doubt."

"He stole cans of food from us," said the old man. "He's a thief."

The old woman grumbled.

"The Party never steals," she barked. "It requisitions or confiscates. It's never theft."

The old man grumbled in turn but added nothing. The sudden surge of dialogue died down for a couple minutes.

A few droplets fell on the glass of the skylight right above, like flying pebbles, then nothing.

"I can give the jar back," said Kaytel after clearing his throat. "I thought you didn't need it anymore."

The old woman turned her head toward her husband. Her eyes remained closed.

"What's he saying, that dickhead?" she asked.

"The pickles," said the old man. "He says he can give 'em back to us."

The old lady clicked her tongue, perhaps as an expression of satisfaction.

"You see?" she said. "The Party proceeds to a redistribution. What it takes, it gives as a gift to the needy. It don't forget people like us."

"That would take the cake, forgetting us!" muttered the old man.

Strummheim had remained mute, perched less than a meter from Kaytel a little above him on the next step up. His breathing had grown calmer but every now and then he let out an oppressed sigh that concluded on an accordion note. Not very loud, but distinct and ridiculous.

"Borgmeister," he suddenly said, then he stopped, and then began a sentence.

He had begun a sentence. The sounds he emitted for a moment recalled to Kaytel the movements of a dreaming dog's mouth, then became comprehensible again.

"I have something to say to you. From Dame Patmos."

Dame Patmos, Kaytel heard.

Damn Dame Patmos, he thought.

"Go ahead."

"It's confidential. Can we see each other in private?" asked Strummheim, pointing down to the dead couple.

Kaytel pouted.

"They can be trusted," he said. "They have convictions. They read the Party's publications."

Strummheim let thirty seconds go by.

"What factions do they support?" he said doubtfully.

There was an empty moment. The rain fell on the building, lashed the skylight, streamed in the gutters, the pipes, lashed, sang.

"What do those two fuckfaces want?" asked the old woman.

"They're policemen," said the old man. "They're starting an interrogation. They wanna know what factions we sympathize with."

"Don't tell them we support 'The Posadists of the Ninth Month'," trumpeted the old woman.

"I have no mind to answer them," said the old man. "I'm not like you. I don't collaborate with assholes."

The old woman moved, then twisted a little to show that she was going to speak to the people sitting above her. Because she was half-turned to them and had raised her nasally voice, Strummheim and Kaytel understood she was now speaking to them and not to her elderly husband.

"We don't support anyone," she said. "We are loyal to the Party and we don't get involved in squabbles among factions. Factions are bullshit."

"Name them one or two of their fucking factions anyway," the old man advised.

"Why?" bridled the old woman.

"So they think there's some point to their interrogation," said the old man.

The old woman protested, then pouted, and finally began to wheeze again in the direction of the policemen. She enumerated a few names that perhaps had had a moment of glory in the Party once, a long time ago, or perhaps she'd just invented them.

"We're against all factionalism that harms the Party," she announced. "But because you seem to care, in our youth we adored 'The Bundists of Ecstatic Radicality,' 'The Intercontinental Red Party,' 'The Horse Butchers,' 'The Virgins with Children.'"

She grew quiet.

"'The Disillusioned with Polpotism,'" added the old man.

"Yeah, those guys, we really adored them," barked the old woman.

Kaytel allowed the last echoes of voices to fade.

"You see, Strummheim," he said. "They're like us. You can speak in total confidence."

29

Then they were silent as the grave for fifteen minutes, half an hour. Kaytel had wedged the stolen jar between his feet—the requestioned Malossol pickles about to be redistributed—and no longer moved. For a long time, Strummheim kept up his heavy, choked breathing, then, after a final accordion-like vibration, no longer emitted the slightest breath. The old people occasionally cleared their throats but no longer conversed about the world and the police.

Daylight had come, but the stairwell remained crepuscular. The din of the rain continued with a regular, rocking rhythm and, if the participants in this scene hadn't been dead, no doubt the sound would have lulled them into a gentle slumber.

"Listen, Borgmeister," Strummheim said when no one in the little group gave the slightest hint of life any longer. "Dame Patmos sent me."

Kaytel nodded. He didn't seem surprised.

"You know her?" asked Strummheim, who *was* surprised.

Kaytel preferred to deny it. Strummheim thought he was Borgmeister. No point in putting an end to the misunderstanding.

"Bah, by reputation," he answered.

Strummheim hesitated; the presence of the two old people still made him uneasy. He nodded for half a minute, considering whether to speak and at last said:

"She wants you to collaborate with her."

"Bah," said Kaytel.

"She knows that you were contacted by a certain Kaytel. You know him?"

"No," said Kaytel.

"He was working for us," Strummheim explained. "On a sensitive investigation. He's been stripped of his functions by the Central Committee. I'm his replacement."

"Okay," acknowledged Kaytel in a neutral voice.

"He's dangerous," continued Strummheim. "He's a lone wolf now."

Kaytel agreed.

"We have to take him out," concluded Strummheim.

With this, silence filled the stairwell for a moment. Strummheim made a sort of theatrical pause, but he also obviously wanted the information to descend from his interlocutor's ears to the depths of his brain, those depths that allow one to understand or accept the world of the living and the world of the dead, their complexities, their chasms.

"I wonder why," said Kaytel at the end of this silence.

Strummheim answered immediately, as if he'd been waiting for this occasion to once again elaborate on the matter and, at the same time, take a weight off his shoulders.

"I also wondered why," he said. "It's one of those practices from another era. But those are Dame Patmos's orders and they're clear. Eliminate the lone wolves, Monroe's girls, the supporters of Monroe like Breton and even you, Borgmeister. Even you."

Kaytel let out an undecipherable moan.

"But if you collaborate with Dame Patmos, the Party will rehabilitate you," Strummheim promised.

"But I was never banned."

"Well, you'll be rehabilitated, it's been planned," Strummheim insisted.

"Before or after the execution?"

Strummheim let some time go by. The rain continued to fall and, in the half-light, it induced indolence and obliviousness. The rain lashed and lashed against the walls, against the skylight, it lashed and then it continued farther down, farther away, to be swallowed up in the end in even darker places, ever darker places. Time, when one thinks about it, mostly follows the same path, at the same speed. Hours went by. The day went by.

Outside, rain, very hard. Almost total darkness in the stairwell. Odors of linoleum, rat piss, and the grungy clothing they all wore.

Kaytel broke the silence.

"Rehabilitation or not," he said, "I'm personally persuaded that the Party is totally fucked. Don't you think so too, Strummheim?"

One step up, Strummheim moved his exhausted body. His features were invisible in the dark. Judging by the sounds of the breath escaping his lips, doubt and discomfort dominated. He took a while to respond.

Finally he said, "What's for certain is that the Party is going through a rough patch."

"Bah, so are we," Kaytel said philosophically.

Silence once again spread through the group. As the darkness grew thicker, one no longer noticed the presence of four motionless individuals on the stairs who were perhaps reflecting on what had just been said, or who perhaps were content to simply wait for nightfall. As for the audio, the rain was a distraction. It surrounded the building and bombarded it.

When night had really arrived, Kaytel put an end to their collective ruminating.

"Not so easy," he said.

It's hard to say whom he was addressing and in what regard. A phrase that opened onto nothing.

Strummheim gave the impression that he wanted to reply, but no sound escaped his lips. He'd suddenly begun to gasp for breath again.

"Are you injured?" asked Kaytel.

"Bah," said the other man.

"Are you injured, Strummheim?" Kaytel repeated.

Strummheim was fighting against the panic in his lungs and then he managed to control his ribcage somewhat and answered.

"A girl in the street shot me," he admitted.

"They do that a lot around here," said Kaytel.

A silence followed.

"You're lucky you made it out," added Kaytel.

Again, a sentence that opened onto nothing.

30

In the middle of the evening, when not another word had passed anyone's lips for hours, Kaytel rose, picked up the jar of pickles, and mumbled to the company that he was going up to the fourth floor. Unexpectedly, Strummheim rose immediately and prepared to follow him. Clearly he had no desire to remain all night in the presence of the old people.

Kaytel started up the stairs that led to the next landing and along the way pressed the light timer button. Despite several attempts, light was not forthcoming.

"He sabotaged it," Strummheim remarked.

"Who?" asked Kaytel.

"Kaytel," Strummheim promptly answered. "Dame Patmos warned me against him. He knows where you're hiding. He's going to try to kill you."

"Bah," said Kaytel.

They arrived at the fourth-floor landing, in front of Borgmeister's apartment.

Strummheim detained Kaytel.

"Wait," he whispered. "What if the other guy is lying in wait behind the door?"

"There are two of us," Kaytel said. "We can neutralize him."

"Dame Patmos didn't talk about neutralizing him," said Strummheim. "She said to execute him."

"Boh," hiccupped Kaytel.

They pushed the door and went in. Kaytel turned on the light. The room was empty. It smelled musty, of clogged pipes. Kaytel scrunched his nose.

"The rain hasn't stopped," he declared. "The ventilation is bad."

He pointed to the skylight. He went over to it and opened it a bit. The sound of the raindrops slapping the windowpane was immediately joined by the thrumming on the roof.

"Make yourself at home, Strummheim," suggested Kaytel unenthusiastically.

Strummheim was not acting like an intimidated guest; rather, he was quite relaxed. He took off his shapeless police coat and, since the only coat hook near the door was occupied by Kaytel's raggedy raincoat, he threw it across the bed, and sat on the mattress facing the door. His breathing sped up for a moment then calmed and, twenty seconds later, it stopped and didn't start up again.

Kaytel placed the jar of pickles on the nightstand. Strummheim was sitting on the spot Kaytel had occupied continuously during the previous days and nights, and this annoyed him somewhat, to the extent that he thought of asking Strummheim to move. Then he decided against it, pushed aside a sleeve of Strummheim's coat that was taking up too much room, and sat down in turn on the other side of the bed. Now he was staring at what was in front of him—the wall with dirty blistered paint and plaster patches.

Their backs were to each other, but without hostility. Simply.

The room was filled with a great calm.

Harsh light. Naked bulb. Sometimes a slight voltage dip, but nothing really of note.

Rain outside.

Sewer odors.

Two motionless men.

The hours passed.

Neither Strummheim nor Kaytel moved, or else ever so slightly as if by mistake, putting an end, for a moment, to their catatonia and their apnea. Then Strummheim half turned toward Kaytel.

"Say, Borgmeister," he said. "How about doing a little exorcism for me in the meantime?"

Kaytel flinched. He'd been startled in the midst of sleepiness.

"An exorcism?" he repeated.

"A purification," Strummheim explained. "In case Kaytel shows up and I have to kill him."

Kaytel let out a long, heavy sigh.

"That's not necessary," he replied.

"You're a shaman, right, Borgmeister?" Strummheim asked.

"Bah, yeah," lied Kaytel.

"It's important to me," Strummheim said. "I've never executed anyone. I'd prefer to be pure to do it so I don't get into trouble."

"What kind of trouble?" Kaytel asked, interested now.

"I dunno," said Strummheim worriedly. "Afterwards. Trouble."

He crossed and uncrossed his arms. Nervously. He fidgeted. The bed creaked under him.

"Listen, Borgmeister," he continued. "You're someone I can tell. I belong to a faction that believes you have to purify yourself before inflicting death on someone."

"Ah," said Kaytel.

"'The Dancing Women of Leninism,'" Strummheim confessed. "Before, it was called 'The Sacred Dancing Women of Leninism.' We wound up shortening it."

"Only women?" asked Kaytel.

"No," Strummheim responded. "You can count them on one hand and, other than Dame Patmos, there are only men."

"Dame Patmos belongs?"

"She doesn't tell anyone. It's a secret faction. But yes. She's a member."

Kaytel shook his head. Damn Dame Patmos, he thought, out of habit but with a strong hint of bitterness. He couldn't understand who this woman was now and what role she still had to play, what role she would still play in his life and in his death.

He returned to his meditative position facing the wall and, for a moment, the two men ruminated about existence in general and, in particular, about their relationships with Dame Patmos and the dancing women of Leninism.

"If you're interested, you can join us," Strummheim proposed.

"Join you where?"

"Join the dancing women," said Strummheim, shortening a little more the name of his faction.

31

It's hard to say what had made him so sure, but in any case Strummheim reckoned that Kaytel had accepted to carry out the purification ritual they'd discussed earlier, and all of a sudden he stood up to get ready.

Kaytel heard him stand and scramble and, when he turned around, he saw Strummheim removing his sweater.

"Hey!" he exclaimed. "What're you doing, Strummheim?"

Strummheim's head and hands were hidden in the folds of wool and he was having trouble extricating them. He bellowed something that resembled a death rattle.

"What *are* you doing?" Kaytel repeated.

Kaytel had jumped with both feet on the floor and was now watching Strummheim's gesticulations with foreboding. The room was not very warm and the policeman had no reason to get undressed, especially not in such disorderly haste, bellowing. At last, Strummheim managed to disentangle himself. The sweater was a vert-de-gris color that suddenly seemed sinister in this wretched room under wretched lighting, and in the disastrous odors of defective plumbing and corpses. Strummheim threw it in a ball, furiously, on his equally wretched coat. All his clothes were stained and encrusted with dried blood.

"I'm getting rid of the superfluous," said Strummheim.

He'd begun breathing again, and his breath was arrhythmical, sibilant, interspersed with guttural sounds lacking all melodiousness.

"You'll catch a chill," remarked Kaytel.

Strummheim was unbuttoning his uniform shirt, its bluish color faded from all the washing, a color that appeared only on the spots not soaked in blood. Then he bent down to unlace his shoes, removed his shirt, opened the top of his trousers, and soon he was there in his underwear, facing his clothes tossed higgledy-piggledy on the bed. Kaytel was watching him with a sort of repressed despair; he felt unable to intervene. All this started three days ago, he thought. It's but a link in a chain I don't control. Something like a dead man's nightmare, like the first chaotic days in the Bardo, the first nerve-racking adventures. Nothing I can do about it.

He didn't know how to behave, he didn't know what to say, and he said nothing.

Next Strummheim removed his undershirt and underpants. His chest had been shredded by two bullets, one at the level of the floating ribs on the side of the liver, the other higher up, on the left. The wounds were fairly clean. You could see parts of organs on the inside. The heart was not really identifiable. In any case, it wasn't beating.

"I'll take off my socks when the ceremony starts," he said. "The floor is chilly and I don't want to catch a cold."

Kaytel hesitated.

"You're nuts, Strummheim," he said.

Strummheim resembled a wounded mammal, not very hairy and depressed.

"Yeah, so what about it?" he retorted.

Kaytel walked around the bed, passed Strummheim, and went to rummage through the closet and drawers. There was an abundance of sorcerer's gear. He gathered the different bells and amulets, put a feather necklace around his neck, slipped on a bracelet with a long outgrowth of hair, and put on a second necklace made up of minuscule skulls, scarabs, and aluminum strips. He was ashamed to play this role of a carnival shaman, so to jettison this shame, he thought about nothing.

He'd turned toward a wall to put his trinkets in order and to try, with some urgency, to imagine the elements of the ritual to come. He was stalling. He didn't look at Strummheim. Nevertheless, behind him he could feel the man's anxious expectation, hear his breathing, staccato or hoarse, and, because he couldn't prevaricate any longer, Kaytel reoriented himself toward the middle of the room.

Beneath the paltry lightbulb, Strummheim was exposing his nakedness most inelegantly. A beer belly starting to form, breasts already deformed, all the physical devastation of a man in his fifties who'd never bothered to keep in shape—pervasive sagging of sad, gray flesh, morose colors, the beginning of the skin's deterioration, red blotches here and there, white blotches, a constellation of pimples around the waist and on the backside, a boil on the left side of the groin. A body neither clean nor dirty. Occupying a large part of the chest, the two wounds formed wide crimson craters and were not bleeding. Open, sinister, but not bleeding.

Unable to stop himself, Kaytel directed his gaze toward Strummheim's genital area. The latter was exposing it to view without covering it with his hands, perhaps because there's a time after death when all sense of modesty disappears. On the whole, Strummheim's sexual apparatus, shrunken from the room's cold, conformed to what can be seen elsewhere on humanoid or human males: it was ugly and grotesque.

Strummheim shivered.

"See, Strummheim," Kaytel observed. "You're cold. Why don't you put your clothes back on?"

Strummheim shrugged. One of his shoulders had a tuft of erratic duvet at the top of the curve—a few whimsical hairs on livid skin.

"Come on, Borgmeister," he said. "Let's get it over with."

Kaytel approached, jingling. He, too, wanted to get it over with. While he was stationed in front of the wall, he'd thought of some sentences that would ring just true and obscure enough for the other man not to doubt that his words were both appropriate and magical.

"I, Borgmeister," he said softly, "come to you so that you will gain back your purity and so that you will be calm."

He waved an armful of feathers above Strummheim's bovinely submissive head.

"I call on the Sacred Dancing Women of Leninism! . . ." he continued. "I call on the Bordigists of Great Compassion! . . . I call on the Sisters of Red Dawn! . . ."

He was concentrating on appearing inspired and fearsome, but suddenly he was so ashamed of the discourse he was using to accompany his magical gesticulations that he lost all desire to speak.

"In the name of the Bolsheviks of Clear Light," he said, then grew silent.

For two minutes he continued to circle Strummheim while waving around feathers, skulls of dwarf rodents, fur amulets, and bells. He didn't even pretend to dance; he didn't feel he could. After three complete circles, he stopped.

Strummheim remained frozen this whole time, hunched over, as if burdened by the weight of his sins. He noticed the pause and complained.

"Go on, Borgmeister," he said. "You can't end the ceremony like that."

"Oh, really? And *you're* an expert in purification ceremonies?" said Kaytel, miffed.

Worried by Kaytel's bad mood, Strummheim shriveled around his wounds. His external genitalia trembled, as if animated by an independent source of shivering.

"It's not done," he said. "We still need fumigations."

"Are you sure?" asked Kaytel. "Fumigations? Come on, Strummheim. Honestly. Do you still feel impure?"

"Yes," Strummheim whispered.

Another series of shivers ran through him.

Kaytel looked around the room to see if he could find something to use to make smoke, hallucinogenic or otherwise. There was nothing of the sort.

"I don't have what I need," he complained. "Not even anything to light a cigarette with."

"I've got a pocket lighter," said Strummheim.

"Where'd you get that?" asked Kaytel with surprise.

"Off a dead man on rue Zinkorine," said Strummheim. "He was lying under a plane tree. At first I thought it was Kaytel, but it wasn't. I rummaged through his raincoat. I took his cigarettes, his lighter. Then a little bitch shot me."

Kaytel went over to the bed and sorted through the pile of Strummheim's rags. His shaman's outfit again produced metallic sounds, bells and amulets accompanied his movements, clanking. Then he was palpating the folds in the coat and soon found the lighter deep in a pocket. He rolled the thumbwheel. A spray of sparks crackled and gave birth to a flame. He extinguished it immediately and shut the lid. If there was still a little fuel left, no point in wasting it.

"We've been reduced to this," he sighed.

"To what?" asked Strummheim.

"Rummaging through the pockets of the dead," said Kaytel.

Now Strummheim was immobile between the bed and the wardrobe, head lowered, shoulders sagging, and he waited stark naked while Kaytel came and went, searching for some ingredient that would send off smoke as it burned without causing a fire.

Pointless search. As a last resort, he eyed one of the socks Strummheim had removed before the ritual began. The bit of fabric would catch fire with difficulty, spread around quite a bit of smoke and once reduced to ashes, it would barely be missed by its owner.

Solemnly he stood before Strummheim, waved the sock around, and lit the lighter's flame under it. The heel crackled for a second. Strummheim let out a braying sound, shoved his arms forward, and ripped from Kaytel the formless bit of black cotton he was holding that, no doubt because it was still damp with sweat, had not caught fire.

"Not that, Borgmeister!" cried Strummheim.

He was shrieking furiously. The sock wasn't burning, but he'd begun to trample it as if he were fighting flames. Then he calmed down and shut up.

Without removing his shamanic rags, Kaytel went to sit on the bed next to where Strummheim had been sitting earlier. He dropped heavily onto the pile of clothes. His bells and chimes trembled for two or three seconds as he spread across his knees his hands of a sorcerer policeman stunned by the turn of events. "Put your clothes back on, Strummheim," he murmured. "It's over."

Strummheim awoke from his stupor, hopped grotesquely while putting on the sock the heel of which had not even blackened but, as if discouraged at the idea of putting on the rest of his clothes, he stopped there. He seemed to reflect, then his gaze grew cloudy and he appeared lost. He took a couple of steps and collapsed on the bed next to Kaytel.

"It's over," Kaytel insisted. "You're purified. You can get dressed."

"I'm fine like this," said Strummheim.

He was once again inert.

"At least put your underpants back on," suggested Kaytel.

"Why?"

"If Kaytel shows up," said Kaytel, "you'll look just great."

"I am what I am," replied Strummheim stubbornly.

32

That's where they were in their conversation when they heard footsteps on the stairs. Someone was coming up.

"Someone's coming," Kaytel noted.

"If it's Kaytel, waste him."

"You said you'd take care of that," Kaytel protested.

"I'm not dressed appropriately," said Strummheim.

Kaytel let out an exasperated sigh and did not insist. More than anything, the atmosphere between the two men was one of despondency. They were the perfect picture of passivity, seated in front of the door, one with the face of an exhausted policeman and the garb of a sorcerer, the other with his clothes off and a perforated body and, on his face, the expression of a brooding brute.

Half a minute went by, then the silence deepened because the footsteps had stopped at the landing. Either the intruder was catching their breath after the climb, or they were wary, and trying to guess what awaited them inside the apartment.

One or two dozen seconds. No movement, no noise. Then the wood door pivoted and a man arrived on the threshold and crossed it. Behind him, the shadows of the stairwell seemed to belong to the black space.

Borgmeister, immediately thought Kaytel. Who else could it be?

In reality, if this idea had come to him, it was out of weariness rather than anything else, out of the childish desire to be done with it as quickly as possible, to be done with everything, the rain, the waiting, death. Because the newcomer hardly resembled the image of Borgmeister that he'd held in his memory until then on the basis of their meetings, discreet, rare, always in poorly lit locales. Back then, Borgmeister looked like a frightened outcast, and he had been an impressionable man, shifty-eyed, bone-thin, dressed in dingy rags, whereas the character standing on the threshold seemed sure of himself and not at all frightened to discover in his house, on his bed, two human-sized parasites who seemed laid low by fear and exhaustion. This person was now a chubby guy in his fifties, with features whose flabbiness was contradicted by a hard, roving gaze that glasses with thick lenses could not soften. His hair or his baldness was hidden under a black leather cap, which would have been the mark of a political commissar if it had been another era. The visor of this headgear was sending drops down the front of his wrinkled, dark blue shirt. He had opened the sides of his cloak that was dripping on the linoleum in the entryway. His face shone with sweat or rain.

All those drops, thought Kaytel.

He clung to the idea, the most logical, that it was indeed Borgmeister who stood before him. But he didn't recognize him.

The newcomer observed the room and its occupants without showing any emotion. He seemed to be accustomed to visions, and even to this vision in particular. He was behaving as if he'd already seen in a dream, in his room, two people seated on his bed, one in a coat, decorated with grotesque necklaces, the other naked as a jaybird, and both with fixed expressions that revealed nothing but numbness. And he cared not a whit.

The first moments of observation having past, Borgmeister ended his immobility and headed toward the bathroom. He could be heard urinating and flushing, and then he reappeared. He had removed his cloak, but not his Chekist cap. He went and stood in front of Kaytel and Strummheim and spoke to them. He addressed them, articulating carefully, as one does in order to be understood by dead people and, for the first time since his days of wandering and stopping in the house on rue Tolgosane, Kaytel felt an existential anguish that constricted his heart. Until then, even if he hadn't totally eliminated the hypothesis according to which he had simply tipped over into the floating world of after-death, he had been in no hurry to believe it. A girl had shot him, he'd been hit right in the chest and, ever since, he roamed the night, in slow motion, yes, and yes, without being sure either of his physical state or of what remained of his consciousness, but he didn't think he'd fallen down too many rungs on the organic ladder.

Well, I'm still hale and hearty, he thought.

So does he think I've tipped over into death, that asshole? he thought.

"Don't be afraid," Borgmeister reassured them. "Continue to make yourselves at home. I'll be here for an hour at most. I'll grab a few things and then be on my way. Stay where you are. Don't move."

"What's that big piece of shit saying?" asked Strummheim, turning slightly toward Kaytel.

"He wants to take a few things," said Kaytel.

"By what right?" Strummheim protested.

Kaytel waved wearily. Strummheim had not identified the newcomer, either because he'd never had the occasion to study his photograph in the Service offices, or else because death had begun to cloud his memory and his mind.

"And anyway, who is that asshole?" continued Strummheim. "Kaytel?"

Borgmeister had no doubt heard the question. He contemplated Strummheim disapprovingly. He stared at his lifeless eyes, then his gaze slid down toward the policeman's crotch, which, in a way that denied all notions of shame or shamelessness, exposed his testicles, his puny cock, and his pubic hair. His disapproval grew.

"No," said Kaytel, relieved not to have to lie for once. "No, he's not Kaytel."

Strummheim reacted. He grumbled something remotely related to Kaytel, the Party, or who knows what, perhaps his burned sock.

"If that's Kaytel, waste him," he said in closing, distinctly.

"I just told you he's not Kaytel," said Kaytel impatiently.

For a moment, nothing happened and not a single word, even an idiotic one, was exchanged.

"I've come from afar," said Borgmeister all of a sudden. "I've come from where you're going."

This idea immediately displeased Kaytel. This *where you're going* was that unrepresentable place from which the Monroe girls had come. At best, one could visualize a long black path, a sooty, bardic gallery where one had to wander for a considerable amount of time before changing worlds, be it in one direction or another. A horribly dark tunnel where loneliness and the worst imaginable crushed you night after night, century after century.

"Don't think I'm going away," Kaytel declared violently. "Me, I'm staying here."

Strummheim spoke in turn. It wasn't clear what had gone through his mind after Borgmeister's *where you're going*. Maybe nothing.

"Where did the asshole say he was going?" Strummheim asked.

"I'm not going anywhere," Borgmeister interjected.

He continued to speak, clearly separating each syllable that came from his lips.

"I'm not going anywhere," he continued. "I'm staying here. There's work to be done. A tremendous undertaking. The Party must be reformed."

"What's he saying?" asked Strummheim.

"He wants to reform the Party," Kaytel explained.

Strummheim showed his indignation by shifting from one butt cheek to the other. His nakedness transformed his movement into a primitive dance. On his chest, on the areas that had not been shredded, the gelatinous part of his breast trembled.

“What if we off him anyway, even if he’s not Kaytel?” he suggested.

“Bah,” Kaytel said with calm.

Borgmeister wondered what to do. Expulsing the dead from an apartment they were squatting is a delicate operation, not always successful. The dead are slow, stubborn, and they return.

Borgmeister wasn’t sure he could force the naked man to get up, then guide him toward the staircase without causing too much damage, and then also send him toward the bottom with an armful of clothes, even if it meant breaking the remains of his bones. He wasn’t sure either that he’d be able to convince the other man, the clothed one, to get rid of his shaman’s skin and return the scarves he’d appropriated, as well as the necklaces and amulets. He might have to rough him up a bit, grab back his things, tangle with him while trying to forget the smell coming off him of assassinated police officer and nomad between night and death.

Or he could ignore them completely and take up his activities as local magi again. He’d manage, with a bit of patience, to get back the disguise and accessories that for the moment were in the possession of one of the two guys. With a little patience. Three or four days.

He swayed from one foot to the other and, after a moment, decided to leave the dead where they were, on the bed. Later he’d see how to manage with their presence.

“But I’m going to stay for a while,” he declared. “I’ve customers to see.”

Strummheim startled. His body shivered again, especially his testicles and gelatinous breasts.

“What, that asshole is still speaking?” he whined.

Shivers of indignation and cold shook him. He was still trembling when Kaytel responded.

“He’s waiting for customers,” Kaytel explained. “He runs a business.”

“A businessman who wants to reform the Party,” noted Strummheim. “We’re really in an apocalyptic moment now.”

"To be precise, this evening I've got a meeting with a woman customer," said Borgmeister.

"A woman, my ass!" Strummheim instantly responded.

33

The woman arrived shortly afterward. She knocked on the door and, without waiting for an answer, came in.

Fuck! thought Strummheim, in the flowery language of the dead. Dame Patmos!

That's all we need, thought Kaytel.

The three men were dumbstruck by the apparition, but for different reasons. All three of them knew her, but their memories of her didn't overlap. Kaytel had known her when they were young, then had recently renewed ties with her when she was responsible for the mission, impossible, of going to kill Monroe in the land of the dead. Strummheim had met her a few days earlier, when she had appointed him on behalf of the Central Committee to the position previously held by Kaytel and had ordered him in the same breath to waste Kaytel. As for Borgmeister, he recalled several extremely discreet contacts he'd had with her while she was carrying out operations parallel to the investigation for which Kaytel was responsible. She'd already come to rue Tolgosane to meet Borgmeister, disguised as a crazy woman who wanted to be counseled and exorcised. She was after Monroe's hide and, well before Kaytel mentioned shamanism to her, she'd asked Borgmeister to go on site, to the other side of death, the other side of rue Dellwo, and fix the problem by making mincemeat of Monroe. Borgmeister, for his part, was hesitant. He didn't feel ready. Dame Patmos had used every trick in the book to convince him to act, and he remembered (not without pleasure) her welcoming flesh, her sexual availability and inventiveness, her perfume, her agreeable, intimate scent.

"Good evening, all," she trumpeted.

She looked wildly happy, hardly disconcerted to find that Borgmeister was not alone: superior, ferocious smile, abundant flesh, powerfully stuffed uniform, massive yet tight skirt, a blouse blindingly white and wide, a plunging neckline that emphasized her irreproachable pneumatic breasts, Stalinian mid-heel shoes and, on her hip, a leather holster to which members of the Central Committee were entitled—an empty pouch, obviously, since carrying a firearm in the psychiatric camp was more or less unthinkable.

She had just removed her yellow raincoat. She walked to the wardrobe and hung it calmly on the only available hanger. She didn't give a good gosh darn that it was wet and dripping. She made herself at home, like a giant sea-lion returning to its favorite boulder after a night-time swim, and with the same slippery movements. The sight of this soaking wet coat suddenly reminded those present that the rain had not ceased, that its hammering had not ceased, that during the minutes and hours gone by, its steady sound was such a part of their universe that its violence and persistence had been forgotten.

"Say, Borgmeister, who are those two?" she asked.

She was pointing at Kaytel and Strummheim. Then she wriggled her unctuous body masses in every direction.

"Not the faintest," said Borgmeister. "Neighbors. They've been squatting here during my absence. Maybe they thought I'd left or was dead."

Strummheim turned toward Kaytel.

"She called him Borgmeister. Did you hear?" he asked.

"No, I didn't," said Kaytel. "Are you sure?"

"No," said Strummheim. "I'm not. I hear everything as if it were coming from very far away."

“Better not to pay attention,” Kaytel advised. “They’re talking nonsense.”

Neither Borgmeister nor Dame Patmos seemed to notice that the guys sitting on the bed were conversing about them.

Dame Patmos had approached Borgmeister.

“You left?” she asked.

She looked for a place to sit down. The chair near the bathroom door did not appeal to her; she began to push Strummheim’s duds out of the way to make room for herself on the bed. Strummheim’s trousers and socks slid to the floor. She didn’t pick them up. Clearly, she didn’t attach any importance to the presence next to her of a naked man, frozen as if in a waiting room or a gloomy sauna.

“I was strolling around the camp,” Borgmeister explained. “I wanted to see just how far the degeneracy had gone.”

Dame Patmos had let herself drop a few decimeters from Strummheim. The bed groaned.

“So?” she asked.

Standing before the bed, Borgmeister answered. One got the feeling that he was now not only addressing Dame Patmos, but all three interlocutors at the same time, this small heterogeneous assembly—a frisky representative of the Central Committee and two dead men dumbfounded by their deaths.

“There’s no going back,” he said. “The camp is doomed.”

“It’s still the only patch where humankind remains,” Dame Patmos pointed out.

“Yes,” Borgmeister admitted. “The last refuge.”

Kaytel intervened. He’d followed the conversation and it seemed to him that no one would be upset if he put in a re-appearance in the room.

“Bah, humankind,” he repeated with a heavy sigh.

“What are they saying, those dipshits?” asked Strummheim.

“They’re saying it’s all fucked,” said Kaytel. “Completely and totally fucked.”

“Ya think?” growled Strummheim.

For about ten minutes, Dame Patmos and Borgmeister conversed. They were engaged in a shared reflection on the endless rain disgorging itself on the last remnants of humanity, on the unclear prospects faced by the Party, on the tasks that needed to be done for the course of History to be reversed, on Monroe, young Monroe and dead Monroe, on their chances of survival if they left the camp and wandered around outside it. They spoke without in the least considering Kaytel and Strummheim, whom they hadn't identified and who had once and for all been relegated to the category of inoffensive nonentities.

At one point in their conversation, the door opened and the old couple from the second floor made their first appearance. To satisfy an inexplicable urge, they had set themselves in motion. They had left their perch in the stairwell and had hoisted themselves all the way to the fourth floor. While for days they'd remained in semi- or total darkness, or poorly lit by the light timer, at the moment they stood at the entrance to the well-lit bedroom, like two actors coming out of the wings a second too early. The naked bulb had been heating up for hours and had reached capacity, dispensing powerful rays that exposed their pitiable clothing, their grubby bodies and faces. They remained stationary then trembled their way to the bathroom and, as if they were alone, let themselves slide down the wall and collapsed, legs extended and bodies slack.

"Someone left the light on," remarked the old woman.

"It's those assholes from the Party," the old man complained. "They don't give a damn about saving energy. They make themselves at home everywhere."

"Don't insult the Party," the old woman protested. "It's dealing with the situation. It's doing what it can so things don't go south."

"Bunch of dickheads," grumbled the old man.

Dame Patmos and Borgmeister had already started up their interrupted conversation again, right next to Kaytel and Strummheim. Strummheim did not take advantage of the fact that he'd been excluded from the dialogue to reestablish his dignity, even by simply putting on his underpants. He remained slumped on the edge of the bed, his skin the color of residents of the morgue when they come out of their casing. Sex organs in a small sloppy bundle, shoulders leaning forward, concave and inert ribcage, glassy eyes. And, at intervals, he shuddered. Kaytel seemed livelier. From time to time he tried to worm his way into what Dame Patmos and Borgmeister were saying by making his shamanic chimes shiver. The beginnings of aphorisms came to mind, but he didn't have the courage to express them with larynx and tongue.

Dame Patmos had just declared she'd given up her senior position in the Party and now was looking for ways to leave the camp, and even the world in general. And so she was asking Borgmeister—who, because he was well-versed in supernatural things, knew how to go back and forth between the world of the living and the world of the dead—to point out secret passageways to her, and to give her advice about the spacesuit she would no doubt have to wear. She begged him to help her with this enterprise, dismissed the idea of desertion that she would let die in her wake, justified herself and cynically sweet-talked Borgmeister, promising to promote him in the police hierarchy and, at the very least, to welcome him again in her folds, between her phenomenal thighs and her generous breasts.

"What's that bitch saying?" the old woman asked her husband as Dame Patmos caught her breath before starting to coo again.

"She's talking shit about the Party," the old man summarized. "She wants to clear out."

"What faction does she belong to?" the old woman wanted to know.

"She didn't say," the old man answered.

"An anti-Party faction," conjectured the old woman. "It must be 'The Anything-but-Monroe' or 'The Autonomous of the Bardo' faction."

"Motherfuckers," the old man stated.

34

Then, events speeded up.

Kaytel, disgusted by the fact that the two chatterboxes were denying his existence, stood, stepped over Strummheim's socks then the legs of the old woman that were partially blocking the entrance to the bathroom, and went to lean over the toilet bowl. He was nauseous. He hiccupped three times, discharging nothing but a long trickle of spittle that was slow in forming and slow to join the brownish water stagnating at the bottom of the bowl.

As he was straightening back up—upset stomach and cloudy brain—he was surprised by a sudden whiff of silence. Dame Patmos's peeping had stopped abruptly. Borgmeister was no longer in dialogue with her. Not a single person said the slightest word.

Intrigued, he stretched half his face out of the bathroom, and immediately saw that the landing door was open again. On the threshold, standing with legs spread so as to assure her a warrior pose, was a young woman of uncontestable beauty, one of the Monroe girls. She was wearing a commando outfit and corresponded to Breton's descriptions. Rebecca Rausch, Lola Schnittke, Lilia Adouldjamani, Mirka Goldenberg, or another one. Her name doesn't matter, thought Kaytel in a flash. She had a sawed of shotgun wedged on her belly and she waved it around, pointing it by turns at anything that closely resembled a living or dead person.

"Fuck," the girl cried suddenly. "I can't believe my eyes!"

She continued to sweep the room in a terribly threatening way, with great ease, with the ease of a born killer.

"Monroe had warned us, but it didn't seem thinkable," she continued. "Shit, it can't be! The Central Committee bigwigs conspiring in an attic to destroy the Party!"

Kaytel wanted to move toward her and explain that his case was different, that he was your basic militant and had no responsibilities comparable to those of Dame Patmos, or even Strummheim and Borgmeister. He took a step and unfortunately his tongue did not respond to his efforts. He began to stammer a slurred sentence, then, as if he felt betrayed by his own mouth, he exhaled an anemic moo.

He was the first to be hit when the Monroe girl began the massacre.

35

"You got a bullet in you, too?" asked the old woman.
"Two," said the old man. "As if I give a fuck."
"Who was that bitch?" asked the old woman.
"A cleaning lady."
"Been needing one for a while," said the old woman.

V

36

Meanwhile, Breton had regained his strength. Perhaps it was the outside air and the feeling that we'd been freed from all constraint. Or perhaps it was physical exercise because, since we'd escaped from the House of Cosmonauts, we'd barely stopped walking. Our little *séjour* at the Waldemar Ward had not lasted long. We took to the road very quickly, afraid of being caught by Kaytel and his minions and then, the hours rolling by without major incident, we felt we were out of danger. There was something irrational about our certainty that the police would lose all trace of us. Perhaps, after so many weeks of imprisonment, the oxygen suffusing the empty streets made us euphoric.

Perhaps, too, repeated contact with the vegetation had increased our natural defenses against adversity, against exhaustion, against fear. At any given moment, Breton would stop and press himself against the plane trees and hug them. I'd set our travel bag on the sidewalk and do the same. We whispered secrets to the trees about our past and future villainies and we spouted long prayers to the world of grasses in which they—plane trees, lindens, larches and others—occupied a royal place. When we peeled ourselves off the bark, new sap ran through our veins and allowed us to continue on our way with firmer footsteps, fewer episodes of apnea, fewer hallucinations, and less vomiting.

"Can you see where we are?" Breton asked me.

"Not really," I answered.

"I have a feeling we've arrived in the Baltimore sector," Breton said.

"If only," I sighed.

We could recognize certain parts of the Baltimore sector, but not all of them. The ones we'd visited in dreams, yes, and the streets where the Monroe girls appeared, the ones that existed in reality and the ones that were not on any map, like the thoroughfares where tramway tracks ran on rue Dellwo or rue Zinkorine, for example—these were familiar terrain to us. As for the rest, our intel, our memories lacked accuracy. We'd no longer ventured north of the camp when the Party removed it from the zones it controlled. There were still some journeys and exchanges, the Party agents continued their medical and ideological tasks, but more discreetly and less consistently, and tourist trips were not allowed to patients of our ilk. It was an immense place where it was easy to get lost. When we needed to speak to Kaytel about the Monroe girls, about their passageways and their hiding places, we took great pains to situate everything in the Baltimore sector. We were intent on obfuscating everything, even if it meant inventing the names of streets or psychiatric wards. The trouble now was that our ridiculous chatter, our memory lapses, and our lies had fused.

"We shouldn't have spouted all that nonsense during the interrogations," I said.

"Yeah," Breton agreed. "That muddled our brains."

"We know approximately where we are, but we're lost nonetheless," I summarized.

It wasn't yet seven-thirty and warm mists of dawn still lingered between the hospital units. We breathed in air that coated our faces with a damp veil, perfumed with bitter-bile acacias, decomposing asphalt, neuroleptics, and human remains.

We'd pushed into a zone bordered with dormitories. They were of all different sizes but basically built on the same military and carceral model, with similar entrance courtyards, lawns that had returned to their wild state, and a few blackened carcasses of vehicles dating from the preceding millennium. And just then, a small empty lot spread out in front of us; at the back of it rose an imposing group of psychiatric buildings the windows of which were, for the most part, blocked off with hard rubber rectangles, tatamis, or pieces of plywood. Once upon a time there were anarchist troubles in the Baltimore sector, and the style of many of the buildings—post-riot handicraft characteristic of the eras of cheap, hasty reconstruction—had not evolved since.

"That could be the Malakassian Dormitory," I said.

"Who knows," said Breton.

The Malakassian Dormitory was one of those sites we'd seen most often in our dreams. We knew it inside and out, always draped in the colors of the night. It's the place Rebecca Rausch had infiltrated while waiting for backup to come get her and take her to what we supposed was the secret base of the Monroe girls.

There was no one around. Grass, tar, animal-skin plane trees, bitter-bile acacias, leaves, puddles, debris bleached by rain, but not a living soul. Not a bird in the sky nor on the rooftops. No aviary agitation in the trees.

There's that at least, I thought. We'll escape bird shit.

We'd always been friends with birds, and from time to time we enjoyed a croaking, cooing, or hooting; the sounds brightened the great silences of the camp, but we hated getting on our heads or shoulders or shirtfronts the droppings of jackdaws, pigeons, or other pooping guests that visited the branches above us.

"Well, there's that at least," observed Breton.

"What?" I asked.

"A day begun without guano," said Breton.

Now we were hiding behind the trees, examining the dead windows of what was perhaps the Malakassian Dormitory. We were trying to guess if Rebecca Rausch was behind those walls, or if we had only dreamt.

"You think she's still waiting for us in the dormitory?" Breton asked.

I didn't answer. I didn't know and I'd just hiccupped. I had a sudden urge to vomit.

"Put on the Bogdanov glasses," Breton suggested.

"They make me nauseous," I objected.

"They're the best ones in daylight," Breton said.

I placed the bag at the foot of the plane tree and leaned over to dig around in it. Among all the equipment we'd brought, the Bogdanov binoculars were most fit for the occasion. I moved the chessboard, the chess pieces, a scarf, and the Hirsch glasses.

"With those, we'll be able to locate Rebecca Rausch if she's here," Breton said encouragingly.

I shut the bag and put on the Bogdanov binoculars.

Breton was now leaning against the plane tree and we turned toward the invisible bowels of the building. With his wildly wide glasses that magnified his forehead and eyes, he truly resembled a cosmonaut sticking his head into the interstellar void.

He remained motionless and mute for one or two minutes. Then he swayed from one foot to the other and twitched. He could see Rebecca Rausch.

She was indeed there. The Bogdanov binoculars allowed one to see her in the present and in the recent past at the same time. They allowed one to know more. The girl had been one of the first girls, if not the first, to land in the camp. She'd looked for a refuge and had been interned here, in a section where the women who were the most seriously affected were held under strict veterinary control. She was in solitary. Conscious, but, despite the bad treatment and the pitiless conditions of incarceration, she had not cracked, she had neither admitted her name nor exposed the reason for her presence in the camp. The medical personnel, exasperated, detested her and bullied her. Nonetheless, as a result of poor communication between the police and the Baltimore sector, her case had not been reported to the authorities, or else just briefly, and with nothing to tie her to the Monroe girls.

“She’s there. She’s waiting for us,” murmured Breton.

“Yes,” Breton confirmed. “She knows we’re going to come and she’s waiting for us.”

Slowly he removed the glasses from this forehead. He was exhausted. I bent over the bag to open it and put back the binoculars, which were above all a disproportionate piece of equipment, hideous and heavy. Once again I was overcome with nausea. I moved away from the bag and vomited up a few drops of bile, painfully and in several spasms.

“It’s the glasses,” I said between two burps.

“Yeah, I know, I told you,” Breton observed. “Those Bogdanovs always do that.”

37

Just as we were crossing the Malakassian Ward courtyard, a man in a white smock came up behind us. We were on his path and, once he'd reached us, he didn't go around us, so he bumped into us. I felt the contact of his bony shoulder on mine, in any case. He must have thought we were stray patients and treated us as if we didn't exist. He trailed behind him the smell of disinfectant, something I prefer by far to the stale stench of cellars and manure that most often accompanies police henchmen. That seemed to bode well to me and, deep down, I wasn't offended by his cavalier attitude. As for Breton, he repressed a gag. He had perhaps been more shaken than I.

The man entered the building and, as he hadn't closed the door completely behind him, we let half a minute go by and then entered in turn. We were in a reception room, or rather in a space of the size and guise of an intake area.

The area was small, glassed in and stuffy. It gave onto a reception window behind which no one sat, and a transparent door, through which we could see a deserted corridor and a few tables in a common room. A nurse came toward us and without greeting us looked us nastily up and down. Then she ordered us to sit on the sole chair and left us, locking the door behind her. After a quarter of an hour someone materialized on the other side of the reception window and asked us to step forward, say our names, and explain the reason for our visit. She was an unpleasant young woman. She was wearing a blue Mobcap, as if she had just come out of an operating room, and a smock that was not properly buttoned. Below the neckline, we could make out the black fabric of a soldier's or gravedigger's uniform.

"Gourgachvili," Breton boldly uttered.

The nurse was not looking in my direction, which didn't prevent me from nodding in confirmation.

"Internal Affairs," said Breton. "The patients in solitary confinement."

The nurse closed the reception window and disappeared. Once again we were isolated from the world.

We had a plan. We had devised it as we crossed the courtyard. It was made up of three main points: enter using some pretext, reach Rebecca Rausch and have her recognize us, smuggle out Rebecca Rausch. We were counting on Breton's improvisational talents to surmount the obstacles. I admired his sang-froid in front of this disagreeable woman. I saw in it his superior chess skills, his tactical talents that always placed my rooks or my queen in jeopardy if, that is, he hadn't already taken them.

Through the windowpane, you could see the corridor that had been painted white three or four decades earlier. At the back, the common room was filling up. Patients were seated, hands resting on cafeteria tables and, in front of them, there was nothing. No plate, pencil, no object, nothing. It was this nothing that they gave the impression of examining. Their necks were twisted, some of them were tensing their arms in inexplicable postures; they didn't move, or barely. Gray nightgowns, gray socks, gray faces. They've recently escaped from the morgue, thought Breton, and, their escape having been successful, they no longer really knew how to take advantage of their freedom.

Every now and then, a doctor would open a door, stick his torso and head in to see what was going on in the corridor, and disappear. A long hour went by like this, with no event of any significance, and then another hour. Breton was dozing next to me. We were tired after a night of vagabondage. A few centimeters from my shoulder, his body relaxed, his breathing grew louder and in thirty or forty second sequences he even snored.

For the moment, our plan was working, given that no warden had emerged in the reception area to kick us out by putting us in painful, unbeatable armlocks. Breton waited patiently and didn't even try to count the hours going by.

"That's the sign we're here to do an inspection," I stated. "That's what's slowing everything down. They're running around back there to hide their dirty tricks. They're afraid of us."

"Bah," Breton commented, not really convinced.

When mid-morning came, another nurse arrived to get us. First she took us into a doctor's office where two minions in white smocks stood waiting for us. I recognized one of them, Chaliapine or Robson—or something that sounded like that—who'd been part of Kaytel's team and who one day, after I'd been beaten up, had taken my blood pressure and given me a shot. The other one looked like him: the same cowherd build, the same odor of a man in contact with animals, the same fat sweaty face, the same stubby but solid hands.

"So, Breton, now you're with Internal Affairs?" Chaliapine cackled.

"He said his name was Boulbachgochvili, or something like that," said the other man.

He showed his tobacco-stained teeth in a cheerful, possibly voracious smile.

I slumped. Suddenly everything was going badly. Our plan, so carefully elaborated, was failing. Despite my sense of improvisation, I remained mute. I'd opened my mouth a little, but I remained mute.

"Don't worry, Breton," Chaliapine continued. "We've talked to the medical team. They were thinking of putting you in a special cold-storage chamber and eliminating you."

"Of cutting you to pieces right here once and for all," the other man added. "Getting rid of you once and for all."

My legs could barely hold me up. I leaned against the wall trying to catch my breath and, since I couldn't manage to, chose to hold my breath instead. I counted slowly, one, two, three, so that at least something intelligible would come to mind. When I'd got to eight, Chaliapine continued his frightening little speech.

"But in the end, the team decided to use you. To spare you and use you. You're a cosmonaut, right?"

"Yes," Breton answered.

"We're going to need you as a cosmonaut," said Chaliapine.

"Or else, you'll be cut to pieces," the other minion cackled like a hyena.

They made us go back down the corridor and we crossed the common room, brushing against the few cataleptics who had been sitting there hours ago and who hadn't given a sign of life since. Still on the same floor, we were next inside an intensive care isolation room for a creature from nowhere.

The medical team that Chaliapine had mentioned and that, according to him, had decided not to cut me in pieces in a special veterinarian morgue, was made up of three people. They all wore sky-blue coveralls that only revealed their faces and protected the rest of their bodies, feet and hands included. The faces were unfamiliar to me even if, obviously, they were associated with a painful impression of déjà-vu, as often happens in the camp when one has been there for decades. Impossible not to have run into them at least once, in the streets or the common rooms, the faces of officers, authorities, head and non-head psychiatrists, torturers delegated to the suffering of subhumans and the insane, to their surveillance, their incarceration, medicated or otherwise, to their slow death, to their accelerated death, to their unpeaceful death. Three people. At the head of the group, a large woman with wide, batrachian features, chinless, with the brutish gaze of a born leader or a psychopath. She must have held a military rank. Then, a scrawny guy with wrinkled, parchment-like skin, skin that was on the verge of tearing, piercing blue-gray eyes and I was convinced he was Ptak, the deputy director of the experimental veterinary labs, or else his twin, also Ptak, supposedly a researcher in xenomorphology close to the Central Committee. And lastly, another woman. Brunette, very pretty: the beauty of a witch. She seemed to be hierarchically inferior to the others—a nursing assistant or a trainee.

Whatever the case, I didn't waste time examining the medical personnel.

Because only their prisoner interested me. It was Rebecca Rausch.

I've said it before and I'm not ashamed to say it again. Thirty years ago, I'd been madly in love with her. And then, she died.

At that point, she'd just come out of bed to protest some treatment or other and she'd battled the personnel who'd wanted to get her back into it. The mattress and sheets were off the box spring, lying in disorder in front of the window. The bedroom reeked of pharmaceutical liquids that had spilled during the scuffle. She was now sitting on the floor, leaning against the foot of the bed with outstretched legs; she was on a breathing strike. Her eyelids were lowered, her face covered in bluish spots. Her lungs remained completely inert.

Deeming that the scene demanded a muscular intervention, Chaliapine went to stand above her, ready to lift her up and throw her somewhere, on the empty box spring or on the chaotic mound of bedding but, before leaping into action, he sought the approval of Ptak, who refused to give it to him.

The military woman turned toward me and asked if I recognized the girl who was suffocating in front of the bed. I shook my head.

"Say, Breton, you're not very good with faces," she observed.

I oriented toward her an expression of feigned ignorance. Then I turned back to Rebecca Rausch. I saw once again the admirable face of the one I'd loved so dearly, the one I'd loved vertiginously and whom I'd never stopped loving despite our interminable separation. That face was ravaged by having passed into death, and by the awful treatments inflicted on her in the Malakassian Ward but, deep down, she hadn't changed.

"She's one of the Monroe girls," the female military person continued. "You participated in tracking her down with Kaytel. I can't believe you don't recognize her little dead girl's mug."

"Well, I don't," Breton denied immediately and vehemently. "I've never seen this girl in my life."

Ptak shrugged aggressively. His mummy face grimaced. When his voice rang out in the bedroom, parched, shrill, it expressed open hostility.

"Cellar," he prescribed. "Cutting to pieces without anesthesia. We don't need this comedian."

"Unfortunately, we do," retorted the military woman from atop her higher position in the hierarchy. "As a cosmonaut."

I sighed then, and as an irrepressible nausea was rising in me, I headed toward the sink and doubled over. A noisy hiccup escaped from me. I remained leaning over for half a dozen seconds. I really wanted to vomit, but I didn't.

"Are you truly a cosmonaut, Breton?" the magnificent witch asked.

She had a long shiny black braid slipping out from under her surgical cap and she flipped it from her chest to her back. I had a vision of a Georgian mountain dweller. It was impossible not to answer this woman.

I stood upright and then spit out a reluctant sentence.

"I've been trained," I said. "I took some classes."

"Fine," said the military woman. "You'll enter into contact with this girl. We've been trying for days, in vain. You're going to dive all the way into her. With simple telepathy or with the glasses. You decide."

"I'm not sure . . ." I said, trying to weasel out of it.

"We'll leave you together," the military woman ordered. "We'll let you enter into contact. All alone like lovers."

Ptak whistled ironically, cruelly. Sinister.

"United in life, united in death," he said.

The lovely witch assistant chortled. The military woman shook her fat face.

"We'll interrogate you in her stead," she explained. "You'd better have the answers."

"And not the same bullshit you've been feeding Kaytel," Ptak added.

The trainee chortled again. I'd felt a tad of kindness toward her, because she had a magnificent face and also because she seemed to have only a secondary role in the team, but now, with her chortles of carceral camaraderie, I found her unpleasant.

In front of us, Rebecca Rausch seemed to have passed beyond the threshold of existence. She still had the same muscular and elegant dancer's body I'd known thirty years ago. She opened an eye that should have been glassy and bloodshot but that was the same intact and marvelous color of our youth, a golden-brown iris in which I would lose myself to the point of delirium and, for a second, she stared at me to establish an intense exchange, reassuring, friendly, sensual even. Then, after this brief flash, she closed her eyelid.

"She's on a breathing strike," I said after a moment.

The military woman approached, bent over the girl, and I took advantage of this to read the name on the tag on her coverall. Borotchkane. She leaned over the girl and blew her breath straight into her face. The girl did not react.

"She'll get over it," Ptak diagnosed.

"She's having her little tantrum, but she'll get over it," Borotchkane confirmed.

38

Rebecca Rausch. The photograph no longer exists, obviously. I kept it religiously in my mind, under my skull, behind my eyes. It hadn't yellowed, it hadn't got lost like some documents do during brutal and nocturnal transfers from one ward to another, it had not been torn up by bandits or guards, not been destroyed during a moment of suicidal despair, no, it had remained there, intact, unforgettable, preserved from the madness of others, protected by my own.

You're standing on a thin layer of snow. I believe—I'm even sure—it was the last snowfall. We weren't used to those cold spells; the temperature hadn't fallen so low for two or three generations. A miraculous whiteness had covered everything in the camp and we were terribly excited by it. We had all dressed too warmly and, at night's end, we'd gone outside. The group had scattered and you had walked with me up to the trees at the edge of the camp. We couldn't see them but, beyond the trees, barbed wire fences separated us from the ruins, that world of impenetrable detritus stretching for thousands of kilometers, endlessly, and that bears witness to the fact that outside of our psychiatric oasis there were, once upon a time, living beings, a civilization with humans, the insane and the sane, and animals.

You're standing on the snow that hadn't been trampled, by us or by others. You're squeezed into two coats, one buttoned over the other, a puff of steam can be made out around your lips as if you were smoking, yet the morning is clear, the sun has risen and the air is already beginning to grow warmer, and one doesn't need to be a weatherman to realize that this extraordinary layer enveloping the landscape is going to melt very quickly. We are conscious of this minute and we are looking at each other.

I'm looking at you. You're smiling. You're smiling at me. Your face is beaming. Sometimes you claimed to have Ybür or Buryat ancestors and your face reflects this; it's very young, firm, sublime, and you're smiling at me. Once again I admire the perfect shape of your lips, your eyebrows, your cheekbones. Once again I stare deep into your gold-specked honey brown eyes. I tell you that I'd desperately love to dissolve into you, I struggle to find the words, wildly, insanely, and you answer me by widening your smile. At that moment it seems to both of us that we've eternity before us. No foreboding darkens our world, we don't imagine that the next day, you'll be killed during a brief outburst of armed violence between Party factions—one of the last.

39

Borotchkane repeats what they're expecting of me. Establish contact with the girl, extract information from her about her origins, the therapies she underwent in her youth, her memories of passing into death if she had indeed spent time there, about her visions, her dreams, and her future plans.

Borotchkane turned toward Chaliapine who, after having hovered over Rebecca Rausch with all his threatening height, had turned back to the doorway, then to Ptak.

"And not only that. We want her to tell us where the other girls are," said Ptak.

"The ones who haven't yet been located and captured," Chaliapine added.

I'd thought he'd had no other role to play than that of an auxiliary, but as it turned out, he represented the police, the on-going investigation still led by Kaytel (that is, if Kaytel had not already been punished for not having obtained any information at the House of Cosmonauts). So he was representing the police and Kaytel, or the police and the Party. In any case, he was putting in his two cents and no one told him to keep quiet.

Again I felt like vomiting, but I held back.

"Did you bring your equipment?" the trainee asked, grabbing her long black braid and flipping it behind her shoulder.

"Yes," said Breton. "The glasses and the binoculars."

"It's borrowed equipment," I said.

"We'll give it back," Breton added.

We looked at each other. With or without the cosmonaut gear, we knew we would soon be in contact with Rebecca Rausch and, while we tried to appear bewildered, something was boiling inside us, warming our heart.

"The bag is still at reception," I said.

Chaliapine's deputy, the second minion of cowherd stature, spoke. Until then he'd remained withdrawn from everything, like a police figurehead responsible solely for security.

"I'll take care of it," he offered.

He left, closing the door behind him. We all remained motionless for a few seconds, then, as if seized with sudden restlessness, Chaliapine and the Georgian witch, then Borotchkane, picked up the scattered bedding and put it back on the box spring, thereby obtaining rather quickly something that resembled a sick bed. Ptak set off to find a broom in the next room and came back. He handed it to me and, since I didn't see why I shouldn't show some good will, I took it and made an effort to gather the shards of glass that had covered the floor near the end table after a scuffle I hadn't witnessed. I pushed the pieces into a corner. Two flasks, a plate in half a dozen pieces, alcohol-soaked compresses, a syringe. My pile was impeccable.

Ptak didn't give a damn about the perfection of my cleaning job. He was crouched near Rebecca Rausch, taking her pulse.

"It's working again," he said scornfully.

"She's recovering?" asked the military woman.

"Yes," said Ptak. "She's a sturdy one."

Just then, Chaliapine's deputy burst into the bedroom and placed our travel bag against the wall.

The room. A space well lit by non-ecological ceiling lamps, a bed, a night table, a barred window blocked by a metal shutter. There was a sink and, in a small adjoining room, a shower and toilet. For a place of special incarceration, it was rather deluxe. Perhaps back in the day it housed Party officers suffering from melancholia or delusional psychosis.

When Ptak had finished his examination, I sat next to Rebecca Rausch. The tiling was warm under my bottom. I smelled the odor of nervous sweat that floated around Rebecca Rausch, mixed with the alcohol that had sterilized the spots where she'd been stuck with needles. Unlike her torturers, who wore coveralls, and unlike me, wearing my usual psychiatric survivor outfit, the young woman was scantily clad. They'd made her put on a hospital gown and graying underwear. I took her inert wrist in my hand. I wanted to show the medical trio and the police duo that I'd begun my work with the patient and that it was time for them to leave the premises.

I smelled their assorted bad breaths mingling above our heads.

They were getting ready to leave the room but before exiting, they approached us as if to sniff us or observe us one last time, as if to verify that we existed truly, and not merely in theory or in dreams. Then they gathered near the exit. There were two doors, one that closed off the room itself and a second one that opened on to the rest of the hospital. In the meantime, in front of the bathroom, medical staff and cops had assembled, quite impatiently, because Ptak couldn't manage to open the lock with the special key that he seemed to be the only one of the group to possess. The military woman grumbled some advice about the way to rotate the key as soon as it was placed in the lock. The xenoveterinarian was getting worked up. Then the mechanism gave, the door opened, and they all poured out of the vestibule. Almost all of them. The witch retraced her steps and planted herself next to us.

I was sitting on the floor looking up at her, holding Rebecca Rausch's hand and, despite the witch's admirable physiognomy, despite the hatred she seemed to send my way, my way in particular, perhaps because I had admired her a moment before with a gaze that she'd considered improper, despite the threat she represented, I felt no fear.

“We’ll be back tonight, Breton” she said, syllabifying in a way that conveyed real malice. “We want precise, reliable information. If not, before the butchering, there’ll be quite a show.”

She tossed her braid and disappeared.

She’d slammed the main door. I heard the heavy lock click mechanically into place.

A moment earlier, I’d had the impression of feeling no fear, but ultimately I stood up, tottered over to the sink, and vomited several small, foul-smelling vomits.

40

Leaning against each other, Rebecca Rausch and I got to know each other again. More precisely, we were trying to get to know each other again. Our reunion wasn't simple. The loving image I had in mind did not materialize. The mad impulse, the dizzying hug, the fusional happiness, the wild words. None of that materialized.

No sound arrived at us from the other hospital units. We were separated from the outside world by a thick door and by the little entrance vestibule. Now, the room was calm. We were also calm. Sitting on the floor, leg against leg, very close to one another. I no longer needed the Hirsch glasses or the Bogdanov binoculars to connect with Rebecca Rausch, my true love, my marvelous lover. I felt her body coming back to life against me, a life that had left her during her breathing strike. After the complicitous wink we'd exchanged when I'd entered the room, she had physically and psychically distanced herself from both me and her torturers. It took her some time to come back. I understood. I'd put my arms around her in a friendly way and waited.

I began whispering in her ear over and over that she was the woman of my life, that I'd never stopped thinking of her and loving her during the thirty years that had just gone by. I told her how I'd witnessed her entrance into the camp, her fall out of death in rue Dellwo. I made a slight digression about the mechanism of the Hirsch glasses. I described my escape from the House of Cosmonauts, our walk to the Malakassian Dormitory. And I added, again and again, that we would escape before evening, as soon as possible, before the return of the witches and the butchers.

Rebecca Rausch did not react, even if her organism had come back to life. Her breathing had returned to a normal rhythm, but she was still catatonic. She remained inert for a good half an hour then suddenly, she startled. Her body was shaken by a spasm. She pushed my hand away and, grabbing onto the bed's metallic structure, stood up. A rapid, almost acrobatic movement.

"Fuck!" she said. "I almost suffocated because of those shithead bastards!"

She walked over to the barred window and hit the reinforced glass with a furious punch, then, after a few wobbly steps, she sat on the edge of the bed and calmed down.

I stood up in turn.

She held out a hand to me, inviting me to sit next to her. Her hospital gown was open, and again I saw her body close up; its color seemed indefinable, here and there a coppery pallor, elsewhere a yellowish gray. Her bra and panties seemed to come from a flea market for farm antiques. In several spots, parasitic half-circles covered with spikes had attached themselves to her hips, her belly. The odor of an athlete in training emanated from her. None of that corresponded to the memory I had of her. She pulled me toward her as if to kiss me but, as I pursed my lips, she immobilized my head between her fingers and prevented that kiss. I felt frustrated but didn't let it show. She wanted something besides physical contact. She wanted a telepathic contact in order to know more about me. Perhaps she'd retained nothing of the summary I'd given her several times during the preceding half hour.

She stared directly into my eyes. The world around us ceased to exist, her gaze unbearably intense. Without the slightest gentleness, without any precaution, she rummaged through me all the way to my soul. The idea of a passionate exchange, tearful and frantic, was now shelved. Rebecca Rausch dived into me with violent mental techniques she must have learned during her death, and she forbade me to answer. Her gaze dug deep and devastated me. I didn't defend myself. I accepted—dumbfounded, no doubt from love but also from weakness, fatalism, and my habit of giving up—this frightening intrusion.

After a few seconds of profound interrogation, the Monroe girl detached herself from me, stood up, and walked over to the sink. She leaned on the porcelain rim and let out a series of swear words.

"Shit, no way! Fuck!" she said, leaning on the sink.

The opening of her hospital gown had become wider. The ties had come undone. I could see the back of her thighs, her back. It was hard not to think of her as some foreign organism. She was muscular, with odd lumps of flesh, bizarre back muscles, and four or five shiny black half sea urchins that seemed quite at ease on her body.

Then she turned around, came back over to me, sat against me without bothering to close up her gown and again she grabbed my head and plunged into me. Once again a few seconds of unbearable, torrent-like penetration. Then she stopped and shoved me away, grimacing, as if I were some horrifying limp object.

The same short sequence recurred several times—she'd seize hold of my depths, widening her magnificent eyes, then push me away abruptly, without the slightest warning and without love. Then she'd leave the bed, walk toward the sink or flatten herself against a wall, sometimes muttering or shrieking an obscenity, sometimes saying nothing, then she'd come back to sit down and, once again, she'd open her eyes fearfully wide and probe me. She wanted to reassure herself that she hadn't misunderstood what she'd sensed in me.

Perhaps her gaze of the ultra-dead allowed her to learn everything about me in a few seconds without my having fastidiously to narrate my personal disaster, my disastrous lack of adventures, my despondent deterioration over three doleful decades, this compendium of spinelessness and passivity that had transformed me into a hopeless zombie. Perhaps this is how she saved me from opening my mouth to justify myself, or to brag absurdly about my minor exploits—my chess victories over Breton, the nasty tricks I'd played on the medical personnel, or my pitiful procrastination tactics with Kaytel and the Party.

Each time, she forced me to freeze for a moment, after which she'd loosen her grasp on my jaws and cheeks and stand up swearing, bashing her fist against the wall or the wiring over the window. I'd participate in these actions by turning myself into a guinea pig or a vegetable. Yes, the Monroe girl sat next to me on the bed, staring at me with her formidable honey-gold eyes, coming and going in front of me while waving her arms around, yes, this woman merged with a distant image of mad love. Yes. However, the more the minutes passed, the less happy I felt, the less I managed to persuade myself that our reunion was resplendent. Already I could not answer the question I'd asked myself when I'd entered the room: did Rebecca Rausch still love me?

We'll need to take the time to get to know each other again, I thought.

We've been separated for too long, I thought.

We have to relearn everything about each other, I thought.

Once again, she had jumped up and stood facing the sink. It must have been the fourth or fifth time.

"Fucking shit, Breton!" she cried. "You're really not my type!"

VI

41

In the afternoon, I explained my plan to Rebecca Rausch. It was a plan lacking tactical niceties. Unblock the window, force open the metal curtain that obstructed it, jump into the courtyard, run like hell and disappear as quickly as possible. The room was located on the ground floor and you didn't have to be a mountain climber to manage it. Next, the easiest thing to do would be to hide until nightfall in one of the Baltimore sector's empty buildings. Given the scarcity of the human population, the lack of density of the living and even the dead, we'd easily find a hospitable dwelling. It would be imperative to act resolutely and silently so that our prison guards wouldn't have time to thwart our escape and send a team on our heels. An elementary plan and, on second thought, the best one no doubt. In any event, I couldn't think of another one.

"It's that or butchering," I declared in conclusion.

"Bah!" Rebecca Rausch commented. "Stop spouting bullshit, Breton. Butchering in the basement is nothing but bluster. They don't even have the equipment for it, those sons of whores."

She went to explore the night table where her things had been stored when she'd been admitted. She undressed, threw her hospital gown on the bed in a rage, and put on a black commando outfit that stank of burning and after-death soot. The sight of her naked body provoked not the slightest desire in me. It in no way matched the reverent images I'd conserved of it, of this body. I had the feeling that, beneath her flesh, her bones were not in their proper place. I'd always seen the Monroe girls at the moment they emerged from their shadows, fully armored, black and shapeless, rather frightening when they fell out of the nothingness into the night and, suddenly, I realized that in another context, in a hospital context, in the reality of the camp, their nakedness held nothing attractive or reassuring. Besides, they harbored parasites more likely to be found on rocks at the seaside.

"We're leaving right now," she said.

I retched. As usual, I felt overcome by nausea and panic when events moved too quickly.

"Well, for starters, what am I supposed to do?" Breton asked.

She looked me up and down, as if she'd only just now noticed my presence in the room. Her face expressed no tenderness. I turned away to hide my desire to vomit.

"A bigger asshole than you I've never met."

I let the insult slide by. I knew that the dead were crass and, in addition, I had such low self-esteem that I was ready to agree with her.

"We're out of here," she said again. "Fuck, I dunno where they put the shotgun I had on me when I entered this shithole of a dormitory. We'll leave without being able to plug them full of lead, the bastards."

"A sawed-off shotgun?" I asked, to show that I was at least aware of lots of things.

"You know anything about weapons, Breton?" she replied immediately.

"Not really, no," I confessed.

"Then you'd do better to shut your little face," she said.

I began to examine how the window was closed. The espagnolette was bolted shut, the lever arm had been removed. I approached the lock and sniffed it. To tell the truth, I didn't know what to do. I jiggled the visible pinion, pinching it between my thumb and index finger, then backed away idiotically.

Rebecca Rausch shoved me aside and, for starters, popped off the cover of the mechanism that controlled the opening and closing of the shutter. You needed a key to access it, but the cover was made of plastic and didn't resist the two perfectly placed punches and the tearing off that followed. Rebecca Rausch turned to me disapprovingly.

"Fuck, Breton!" she whistled. "What are you waiting for? Barricade the front door!"

I ran out into the small corridor. With the broom and the sweepings from earlier, I improvised a proper sabotage. A few remains of rubber, compresses, and glass shoved into the lock as a plug, the broom handle wedged on the floor between the bottom of the outside door and the entrance to the bathroom. I quickly went to vomit and urinate, then came back into the room, shut the door again, and pushed the bed in front of it.

I'd scratched my hand on the debris. I brought it to my lips, both to lick the wound and because I was waiting for a sign of compassion, no matter how small, but Rebecca Rausch was not interested in what I was doing. She wasn't looking at me, she was given over entirely to her task and she muttered an uninterrupted stream of curse words. She'd just taken apart the shade from the lamp on the night table and was attempting to extract a wire to put it in the pinion of the espagnolette and open the window. She'd already managed to make the electric mechanism of the shutter work to raise it and, on the other side of the wired window, we could now see a row of trees and, behind it, the avenue and its gray buildings that represented our freedom.

Then the window opened with a jolt and Rebecca Rausch turned to me.

"Do I bring the bag?" I asked.

"Fuck your fucking bag, Breton," she said. "We're vamoosing. Get cracking, will you? We jump outside and run."

42

Evening came.

Our escape had been a success.

For hours, we'd zigzagged through the Baltimore sector, wanting to put as much distance between us and the Malakassian Dormitory as possible while complicating the task of any possible trackers by our irrational route. Occasionally we'd stop to make sure that no evil entity was chasing us. This was also an opportunity for me to catch my breath because, even if Rebecca Rausch had realized that I couldn't move at her sprinter's pace, she raced along at breakneck speed. Scampering to keep up with her exhausted me. As night was falling, a downpour began. We sheltered from the rain in an empty building; we had plenty of choices since the area seemed abandoned. I'd taken the initiative to push open the door of this one, on which a marble plaque announced that it had once been an Oncology Institute for Soldiers' Wives and Workers' Widows, and Rebecca Rausch had followed my lead without protest. We'd gone up to the third floor and from there surveyed the surroundings, the deserted avenue, the very black trees in the night, the asphalt with its spluttering puddles, the badly lit courtyard of the dormitory opposite, it too, derelict and lightless. No wind. A mighty rain was falling vertically with the continuous splash of a waterfall.

"Fuck!" Rebecca Rausch growled. "It does nothing but rain in this shitty camp."

"It seems that it's worse in other places," Breton observed.

"No, bro, not everywhere else," Rebecca Rausch corrected me.

"I meant, in the land of the living," I ventured.

"*Fuck you,* Breton," Rebecca Rausch hissed.

The fact that she was using a dead language didn't impress me. I suppose that, like all of us, she couldn't say much more in Church English, a language forgotten for centuries. I took it as a simple linguistic affectation from the beyond, one more obscenity but without any specific intention. Perhaps by this she'd even meant to establish a wee complicity with me instead of bombarding me with filth.

I went to press myself up against the window again. I wasn't thinking about much but I forced myself to reflect. There were miles between us and the Malakassian Dormitory. A great distance, and we hadn't left any clues along our way. No scarf caught in the bushes, no personal object tossed on the sidewalk, none of those elements that denounce the passing of fugitives and that nudge the trackers toward the right path. In fact, we had nothing of the sort on us. My pockets were empty, Rebecca Rausch was practically naked. In addition, I reflected, we hadn't gone through any bushy places. Even if Chaliapine and the others had sent a team to hunt us down, they had no reason to come smoke us out here. This idea cheered me and, my forehead leaning against the glass, I started to hum snatches of shamanic or revolutionary chants.

"Shut up, Breton!" Rebecca Rausch cautioned. "You'll attract the cops with your lamentations!"

I shut up. In truth, Rebecca Rausch had changed her attitude toward me. In the Malakassian Dormitory, our reunion had been disastrous because of the prison context and the urgent situation, but also perhaps because, after thirty years of separation, the wings of our couple were clipped, as Breton would have said. At the time we'd jumped through the window, I'd been persuaded that our amorous relations had fallen to zero. But then, in the state of nervous exaltation that our headlong flight aroused and the sense of freedom that accompanied it, I felt hopeful again. Because there, outside, Rebecca Rausch had calmed down and softened up. She was changing her behavior toward me. Even during the first four or five hundred meters, so decisive, she'd been careful not to leave me behind. Even if I was physically pathetic, she accepted my presence as a co-escapee. Later, when I would feel faint, practically suffocating, she'd pull me behind a tree or a wall and halt for a moment, pretending to believe we'd stopped moving ahead not in order to rest, but rather to examine our surroundings and verify that no one was on our heels. And she'd not objected when, with raindrops exploding on our faces and the streets smelling of damp and storm, I'd decided to enter the Oncology Institute. She'd followed me in total confidence. And now that we were dry and apparently out of danger, she was speaking to me without the hate-filled sharp tone that had marked our first conversations. Or else, when she'd overdone the insults and profanities, she'd come to pat me on the chest by way of an apology and would laugh. I immediately would second her, spinelessly, in her laughter. Let's just say that this was how we'd established relations that were approaching camaraderie. According to Breton, in any case, it was better than nothing.

She joined me at the window. The intensity of the rain had not abated. The night was noisy, the landscape lit here and there by pitiful streetlamps but, on the whole, all was black.

"Shit, Breton," she said. "How could you stand thirty years of this without dying?"

I would have liked to question her about the meteorological conditions of the beyond, about daily life in the black space, about her stages of preparation before the dive into the camp, about Monroe over there, about the atmosphere among the dead, but I thought twice before speaking and, in the end, said nothing. I answered her questions about insignificant things, about material matters and, when she spoke, I listened. I gently foraged for information about her mission, about the Monroe girls, about the future of humanity according to Monroe. In sum, we'd begun a normal conversation.

In sum, we'd got to know each other again.

We'd decided to wait for the rain to abate before going to rue Tolgosane. It was one of the rendezvous spots that had been assigned to the Monroe girls before their departure. Rebecca Rausch had consulted maps, blueprints, and a series of photographs but, according to her, there was no equal to a guide like me, who knew the camp in its most up-to-date configuration. I didn't argue with her, obviously. I knew that I might have some trouble finding rue Tolgosane at night in the rain, but I gladly accepted the role of specialized urban scout that she'd entrusted me with. And I accepted it all the more enthusiastically because it seemed to me that there was something permanent about this role. In this way we wouldn't leave each other, Rebecca Rausch and I, and I could accompany her in all future adventures, whatever they might be, as if we were an old couple.

"I'll stay with you until the end in any case," I suddenly declared with naïve pride.

"What end?" asked Rebecca Rausch.

I hesitated and cast a questioning glance Breton's way. He didn't know either how to respond without making a fool of himself.

Rebecca Rausch's mission was to unfold in several directions and it had several degrees of importance, from the most futile to the most epic.

Some of the guiding principles:

Re-establish contact with the other girls.

Develop with them a plan of action adapted to the circumstances.

Procure the necessary weapons. Do not procrastinate, zoom into action as quickly as possible, execute the deviationists and the traitors of the Central Committee, seek out their allies in the lower echelons and waste them as well.

Prepare Monroe's return. To do so, clean the appropriate Party offices or buildings.

Call a special Convention, re-establish the Party's operations on a sound platform. Rely on the remains of supporting factions such as the "She-Wolves of Non-Duality," "Proletarian Obstinacy," the "Instant Illumination" group, among others.

Resume the course of the interrupted world revolution. Call the youth to the rescue. Encourage the creation of worker and farmer commissions with unlimited powers. Eliminate the camp borders in order to spread the revolution to all the territories that had escaped the apocalypse.

"And what about me in all that?" asked Breton.

"If you don't fuck up, we won't shoot you," Rebecca Rausch promised.

43

On the second floor of the Oncology Institute we'd found closets filled with medical lab attire. Some of the outfits dated back to the period when the personnel had to confront, outside, lethal particles raining down or dust and ashes blown by the wind. That tells you something about their obsolescence.

Rebecca Rausch rummaged in the cloakroom for a minute. She chose for herself a poncho made of thick military plastic colored a hideous green, with a huge hood that, once pulled over the face, allowed you to see through a transparent flap. The antibacterial mask and filters were missing, but it didn't matter. With her black ninja coveralls underneath, the outfit looked good on her and we didn't have to move about under hostile sprays of pathogens or sarin.

I was wet, my detainee clothes were not exactly the freshest, and there were uniforms for the operating room on shelves; still I hesitated to undress in front of Rebecca Rausch and, in the end, I decided not to change. I'd taken down from its hanger a long-sleeved work tunic of blue oilskin, unisex no doubt, and whose waterproofness attracted me, whereas the other lab coats on offer were all made of cotton. The tunic wasn't my size, it fell all the way to my calves and my hands disappeared inside it but, once again, it didn't matter. If I could dig up some headgear to put on top, I'd be equipped for expeditions in the rain. I looked for a while and managed to unearth a vinyl hat approximately my size.

I don't know what I looked like in this get-up and I paraded for half a minute in front of Rebecca Rausch in the hope she'd utter a positive comment. No such comment was forthcoming.

Already we'd left our way station, already we were penetrating into the night. The rain had not let up and we could have waited a little longer, but Rebecca Rausch had had enough of watching out the window without seeing a thing, and she'd decided to go out come hell or high water.

I couldn't say what time it was. It was late. We walked on the very badly lit sidewalks along the boulevard Wundersee. We formed a slightly burlesque looking couple, a woman enveloped in what, from a distance, must have looked like the uniform of an extraterrestrial warrior, and a mental patient lost inside periwinkle blue oversized rags, his head protected by some transparent thing shaped like a jellyfish. As a security measure, we stopped frequently behind the trees and examined our surroundings suspiciously, checking that we hadn't been followed and that no patrol was hiding in ambush farther along to verify our identity. We trudged beneath the deluge, and most of the time waded straight through the puddles. Hundreds of raindrops thrummed on my hat every second, millions of drops bombarded everything around us. The noise was deafening.

Just then, Rebecca Rausch spoke to me. Because of the racket, and also because she was talking through her transparent flap, I didn't understand a word she said.

"What did you say?" I asked in a panic, aware she wouldn't appreciate having to repeat herself.

"The feeling we're heading back to the Malakassian Dormitory. Fuck!" she shouted.

She wasn't entirely wrong. We'd left boulevard Wundersee to maneuver among the black water that pooled along the rue des Sept-soldats, the rue de Clé-pouilleuse, the rue Eberlein and, indeed, on a map of the camp, one might have concluded that we were approaching the large psychiatric compounds but, in reality, we were not on the wrong track and we were progressing toward our goal.

"We'll get to rue Tolgosane soon!" I reassured her, shouting to make myself heard.

"About time!" she screamed.

"Don't be afraid!" I took the liberty of saying.

"Fuck you, Breton," she screamed, without turning her head to me.

Rue Tolgosane was one of those meeting places where, during her training, she'd been told she could find other girls, reevaluate with them their priorities for action according to the circumstances, and maybe even stock up on weapons and munitions. Apparently there was a shaman there capable of establishing contact with the dead and Monroe. At least that's what she gave me to understand. After she'd entrusted this information to me, I'd gone to explore the ground floor of the Oncology Institute. Breton then whispered to me that he in no way believed in the powers of this shaman, that he was more likely a police informant and represented a real danger to us. We'd gone back to Rebecca Rausch to warn her. Our explanations were received with such condescending amazement that we didn't finish our sentences which were, it's true, rather confused and stuttering. I had nothing more to add to the subject. Because she'd decided to go to rue Tolgosane, we'd go there. I wasn't the one in charge.

Then we were on rue Tolgosane.

There were several possible houses and, despite the dark and the blinding cascades, Rebecca Rausch headed directly toward number 27. She'd learned for months, perhaps even years, how to recognize places from photographs or sketches. She knew exactly where she was. I followed her.

Once the front door had been closed, we let our eyes grow accustomed to the half-dark while our clothes shed their water. Rebecca Rausch tipped her extraterrestrial's hood back and I took off my dripping hat, shook it the way one shakes blood off a sword, and placed it back on my head. The entrance hallway smelled of damp, a bit like a secret spider wallow, and a lot like wood covered in mold, cellar fungus. Facing us was a door that must have led to a small courtyard. On our left, a dark staircase.

Already Rebecca Rausch had stepped onto the first stairs.

I followed behind. I dragged my hand along the wall in order to have a vertical reference point. My fingers touched a switch.

"There's a light timer," Breton announced.

His voice faded among the continuous drone of the rain that was amplified by the stairwell that acted as a sound box. I didn't wait for Rebecca Rausch's recommendation—to light or not to light—and I pushed the electrical button.

And there was light, more sinister than the dark, for now we could see the dilapidation of the stairwell, the peeling paint of the walls, the filthy floor.

An old man and woman were sitting side by side on a step, in the staircase that separated the second floor from the third. Their faces were ashen, exhausted, and their clothes were in tatters, soiled with huge stains. Oil, perhaps, or blackened blood. They were hunched over and it was obvious at first glance that they were in very bad shape. Rebecca Rausch had stopped at their level. Breton joined her. For several moments, everyone remained silent, then Rebecca Rausch spoke in a tone I'd never heard from her, very deep, and in a language I couldn't identify and that frightened me. She linked together syllables that contained gutturals and very long vowels. A few sentences. Then she was silent, as if waiting for an answer to a question she'd formulated.

Silence descended on us once again, amid the thundering rain that had overtaken the world. The light timer died. Breton went to push the switch then came back next to me and Rebecca Rausch.

"What's that gibberish she's saying?" asked the old woman.

"She's speaking in the language of the dead," said the old man. "She says she saw us over there in photographs. She says she's counting on us to turn the Party around. She says the Party has collapsed."

"Total bullshit," the old woman spat out. "As if the Party needed us to collapse or to turn itself around."

Rebecca Rausch began her speech again. As a shaman and a schizophrenic, I had in my head several moderately human dialects, but that one seemed awfully incomprehensible to me.

"She must be one of the girls who used to go upstairs to see Borgmeister," the old man reflected.

"I thought that one was done with all that flurry of activity," the old woman observed. "I thought he was no longer in a state to receive young women."

"She says that Monroe will come back to wake up the masses," the old man translated.

"You understand the language of the dead?" said the old woman skeptically.

"A few words," said the old man.

"How about that!" exclaimed the old woman with tender admiration. "You hid that from me!"

She held out her hand and touched the old man on his arm. The old fellow nodded a little, perhaps flattered or moved. An old couple. They didn't give a darn about our presence there.

Rebecca Rausch leaned over them and murmured I don't know what for quite a while. She stopped, perhaps to let her words penetrate the slower brains of the old folk, then she began again, articulating carefully, still speaking the same lugubrious mumbo-jumbo from beyond the grave. When the light broke off, Breton took three steps in the dark and brought it back to life. I said nothing, simply witnessed the scene like a sleepwalker. Rebecca Rausch in her post-apocalyptic slicker, speaking to two tatterdemalions in unintelligible terms, while outside the downpour howled incessantly and, every now and then, the light timer misbehaved, obliging Breton to cross the landing to grope against the wall.

"She's dripping on the stairs," the old woman remarked. "Dribbling everywhere."

"I don't believe what she says," grumbled the old man.

"Well, she's bullshitting piffle," the old woman confirmed.

Rebecca Rausch sighed with exasperation. She turned toward Breton.

"Fuck!" she exclaimed. "We are at 27 rue de la Tolgosane, aren't we?"

"That's what it says above the entrance," said Breton.

"So we didn't make a mistake," she declared. "Those fucking old people are worthless. It's the fourth floor that matters."

She took off her khaki poncho and threw it carelessly in a corner. Breton wondered if he should do the same, but he didn't imitate her. He'd got used to his giant jacket and, even if the sleeves hid his hands, he wound up thinking that it suited him and, in the event of bad weather or unpleasant encounters, it could always be useful. Rebecca Rausch climbed around the old people up to the third and then the fourth floor. Breton followed behind.

We paused in front of the door to the apartment below the eaves. It stood ajar, but we couldn't make out anything inside.

The light timer went out again.

Rebecca Rausch swayed lithely from one leg to the other. She was preparing herself for anything.

The sound of raindrops on the roof canceled out all the other sounds, canceled the creaking of the boards on the landing when Rebecca Rausch changed her supporting leg, erased our breathing, Breton's hiccups and anxious gulps.

"If a brawl breaks out, perhaps I shall remain on the landing," I whispered cautiously.

"Fuck you, Breton!" wheezed Rebecca Rausch, pushing the door with a thump.

She immediately turned on the light in the room. On the floor lay bloody clothes, plaster debris, cartridge casings, and what I recognized as the vestiges of a shamanic ceremony: mangled feather necklaces, scattered colored beads, pieces of charred wood, a punctured tambourine. Bullets from shotguns or revolvers had dug craters in all the walls. The skylight was broken, water dripped in from the roof forming a small stream that flowed under the bed and disappeared into the bathroom.

Breton entered in turn.

"And I talked about a brawl," he commented.

"For a brawl, this was some brawl!" I added.

"Shit! And this was supposed to be a secure spot," Rebecca Rausch lamented.

I bent down, gathered a few beads—blue-green, turquoise, sky blue, navy blue, a few feathers. I stuffed them all in a pocket.

"Why are you doing that?" asked Rebecca Rausch.

"As a souvenir," I explained.

"That's looting the dead," Rebecca Rausch scolded.

We'd already shut off the light behind us, closed the door again, and were heading toward the street. On the second floor, the old folk grumbled. Rebecca Rausch turned to them and said something to them in the jargon of the dead.

"What's she saying?" asked the old woman.

"To go fuck ourselves," the old man translated.

"What a whack job," said the old lady. "She's not even alive."

Rebecca Rausch took the cape she'd left before going up to the fourth floor. Before she put it back on, she shook it vigorously in the direction of the old couple.

The old man wiped his face.

"The Party has gone way down hill," he said. "It's attacking the little guy."

"Don't say that," the old woman protested, wiping her face as well. "That's playing into the hands of the reactionaries."

"Reactionaries, my ass," the old man retorted. "She splashed me on purpose."

Rebecca Rausch had finished putting her cape back on.

"Fuck you, shut up!" she cried in the unholy dead language.

We descended the last flight of stairs and, once in the entrance hall, Rebecca Rausch decided to go take a look at the little courtyard. She pulled the creaking door toward her and the noises grew louder. The crackling of the rain was amplified by the steep walls of the place. The water rushed toward a black, bubbling pool, where it slapped across trash cans filled to the brim with fresh garbage and rags. It plugged away at them, at the decomposing unnamable. Near the drain floated a rather fat shape, with limbs. It was hard to see, everything was very dark, and the waterfalls were obscuring the space. It wasn't an animal shape, so it had to be human remains. Its back was turned to us. No clothes, the legs disappearing behind a plastic bin, the flesh smooth, dark brown or black, with bizarre, sooty plaques and, in several spots, bristly protuberances. The shaved head was hidden in the crook of an arm, drowned, the face invisible. I had the feeling it must have been a woman. I was dying to speak. I had to say something.

"It looks like a girl, poor thing," said Breton without thinking much.

"That's Lilia Adouldjamani," said Rebecca Rausch.

"Lilia Adouldjamani?" I exclaimed.

I hiccupped. Lilia Adouldjamani, one of the Monroe girls. I'd always imagined that the Monroe girls were invincible or, at least, that they couldn't die.

"Of course they can die," said Rebecca Rausch.

Breton had leaned over to vomit up a spoonful of spittle mixed with bile. He stood.

"You can read my thoughts?" he whistled.

"Not always," Rebecca Rausch clarified. "But just then, yes. Shit, it was as loud as if you'd spoken."

The two of them remained for a moment in silence, on the threshold to the little courtyard right next to the waterfall, contemplating the half-submerged corpse of Lilia Adouldjamani and the trash cans from which stuck out a sock rolled over a gray calf, the remains of a coat, human flesh. I'd withdrawn all the way to the stairway. I had trouble catching my breath. After about ten seconds, I went back over to them.

When she'd finished paying silent tribute to her comrade, Rebecca Rausch walked through the rain and bent over near the corpse. She turned it part way over and seemed to be rummaging in the water that the raindrops pinged ceaselessly. When she stood up, she held a dripping object, a sawed-off shotgun over which Lilia Adouldjamani had folded herself the moment she died.

And the ammunition? I thought.

"Mind your own business, Breton," Rebecca Rausch scolded.

44

Rebecca Rausch had no desire to confide in me. But she grumbled at every opportunity and cursed her mission that didn't correspond, in the field, to what had been planned for her. I learned several important things.

The Monroe girls were not immortal. Their hours were numbered, like all other living creatures, even if they'd managed to extricate themselves from the black space where they'd been confined after dying. They'd left the beyond, they'd returned to the camp, but after they'd finished their mission, which was to set the Party back on track, once again they would be condemned to death.

"And I don't find that amusing one bit, fuck!" Rebecca Rausch said.

She considered herself an ordinary soldier who'd been sent to the frontline. All the girls thought they were serving as cannon fodder, destined to disappear so that the Party leaders could reach their apotheosis; this idea had been drilled into them during their training period, but Rebecca Rausch had trouble accepting that Lilia Adouldjamani had been eliminated so soon. She'd begun to suspect that the preparation they'd received over there had been half-assed. That their physical ability to resist the nightmare into which they'd been sent had been overestimated.

"She was the best among us, the sturdiest," she deplored.

She was worried. Although she hadn't examined Lilia Adouldjamani's remains, she was convinced her comrade had not been assassinated. She had died a natural death, overcome by sudden weakness perhaps; as had been explained to them, this could happen without warning, from the total exhaustion of all organic functions. They'd been told it was extremely rare.

"Extremely rare, my ass!" she inveighed. "If we're all like her, we won't last long in this fucking hole!"

I began to think about death. It was a question we rarely raised, Breton and I. The idea of life made us vomit. It returned constantly, this idea, and it startled us, fueled our hiccups and the various fluids we coughed up. It was extremely difficult to live, to survive, to continue this long passage through the universal madness, the universal schizophrenia of the camp, to face the hostility of all and sundry day after day. It was extremely difficult and pointless to take part in this slow obstacle course, to sense within ourself deep mental and physical decline, to feel our bodies grow exhausted, overcome with awful pains and awful smells. It was extremely wearisome to be obliged to move forward at all costs, with at most the perspective of a next step, a next chapter in a book whose end escaped us and would always escape us. Extremely difficult, thus painful, pointless, and punishing. Death for us was merely a neighboring territory into which we'd venture naturally, during our shamanic trances, with or without Hirsch glasses, a territory that, in the end, appeared to us like an unimportant dream and then disappeared, and from which we gathered the shreds of information we hid from the police and the Party torturers. A familiar territory, but nothing more, because all we could make out was the first few meters of a short footbridge that only allowed others to move toward us, the dead toward the living, and it's true that, about this black and floating territory where so much was going on, where leaders like Monroe were plotting the future of the camp, the future of the Party and the future of the living, we knew almost nothing, we knew only the infinitesimal part that served as a vestibule, and not even, simply an exit *from* the vestibule toward the living and their psychiatric camp. Death thus did not really exist for us and, in any case, never had we imagined going there for good. Breton, if ever he began to speak about it, would refuse to imagine its slightest detail and would finish his sentence vomiting. I would begin hiccupping in turn, asking him to move away from the window and return to a game he was complicating by increasing the number of bishops and sometimes even giving the king the same exorbitant powers as the queen.

Other information filtered out from the foul-mouthed mutterings that peppered Rebecca Rausch's monologues.

There were, according to her, at least two weapon caches in the camp, at addresses she did not share with us and that I tended to think of as more oneiric than real, dating back to a revolutionary period that had been totally forgotten, even by the most radical factions of the Party. I was convinced that, once there, she'd find nothing but an arsenal that rust had transformed into crumbs, or empty premises.

She also mentioned sites she called "emergency intermediary reunification sites," where she believed she'd find more of the Monroe girls, whose names she mentioned openly because she was aware that Breton had witnessed their birth out of death and knew them. I recall them here: In addition to Lilia Adouldjamani, whose corpse we'd just abandoned on rue Tolgosane, she hoped to get back in contact as soon as possible with Viola Mourmansk, Mariana Magadane, Cora Kliff, Lola Schnittke, and Mirka Goldenberg.

In the meantime, however, she wanted us to return to the Malakassian Dormitory to get even with the jailers, torturers, and psychiatrists who'd ministered to her.

45

At dawn, when the Malakassian Dormitory came into view, the rain had paused and, just as we were watching the building to prepare our assault, the downpour began again with as much vehemence as the previous night.

Despite the deluge, Rebecca Rausch had given up wearing her poncho that was supposed to offer protection from irradiated or poisoned terrain. She deemed it not up to snuff for her military operation plan, which was to burst into the hospital and shoot left and right, and definitely did *not* include gesticulating in Martian clothes with slow-motion movements and arms hampered by heavy greenish plastic flaps and folds. She took the poncho off suddenly and threw it at the foot of the plane tree behind which we were more or less hidden to spy on the place, and now she was like an elegant female ninja, without the balaclava of course but in black, body-hugging fabric and, even if I'd already admired this outfit when we were running through the streets and again when we had spied at night through the windows of the Oncology Institute, I couldn't help but let out a sigh of dazzled dreaminess. She noticed and gratified me with a furious glare.

"Fuck you, Breton!" she said. "You know I'm not your type!"

The rain had already poured over her and soaked her outfit, accentuating here and there the bizarre shapes of her body.

I bent down to pick up the khaki poncho. I'd just realized that my oversized jacket forced me to contort myself so that my hands could stick out of my gigantic sleeves, making me a military aide unworthy of my comrade. The poncho would also cover my limbs, but at least I'd have the impression of wearing a get-up more suited to the people's war we were fighting. I let my freakish, waterlogged blue smock drop to the ground and slipped into the outfit meant for strolling through a polluted zone. With the shiny vinyl hat on my head, I had the feeling I would at last play a useful role in the plan to revamp the Party and the world. I would have wanted to share this feeling with Rebecca Rausch, but she was no longer by my side. She'd moved away from the plane tree and was running toward the entrance of the building.

We would have liked to mow down a few of the nurses and administrators, starting with the trio of Ptak, Borotchkane, and the Georgian witch but, once we'd crossed the vestibule, we didn't meet a soul. The dormitory was empty; its beds were not messy, but looked like they'd been gathering dust for months. In the common rooms, the stench of piss and madness had faded. The laboratories had been cleansed of all traces of recent research. Everything was unplugged, the sinks were dry and clean, the cabinets contained not one single vial. The room we'd escaped from didn't seem to have housed anyone for the past year. Breton went to urinate in the adjoining bathroom and flushed. The water had been turned off.

For a good fifteen minutes, we walked around the dormitory, exploring the rooms one after the other. It was as if the place had been abandoned ages ago.

"Fuck!" Rebecca Rausch said at last, waving her shotgun around at nothing. "They shoved us into a fucking bad dream, the bastards!"

46

It began like that. With the total disappearance of the living or the semi-living or the dead around us. It began in the Malakassian Dormitory, completely devoid of its usual occupants, penitentiary personnel, medical aides, and women incarcerated for schizophrenia or organic dissidence. No corpses anywhere. An absence of bodies as far as the eye could see. In the crepuscular light of the morning downpour, we paced up and down like flustered zombies, repelled by the echo of our own footsteps; we even opened closets in the hope of discovering corpses or even half-carcasses, the remains of butchering. But nothing. Nothing. And the constant deluge for a soundtrack, punctuated by the furious exclamations of Rebecca Rausch. For a good fifteen minutes. Let's say twenty.

Then, when Rebecca Rausch yelled to me that we weren't going to freak out over so little and that we'd head out in the direction of the House of Cosmonauts, the emptiness continued even after we'd left behind the building and then the Baltimore sector. Everywhere the same nightmarish assessment—not a soul in sight, the patient population nowhere to be found, uninhabited spaces, the police absent even at the station, the Party vanished.

"If it keeps up like this, we'll have a bit of trouble mobilizing the masses," Breton took the liberty of commenting.

"Shut the fuck up, will you!" Rebecca Rausch said, exasperated.

As if I'd spent my time jabbering sarcastically next to her, whereas I'd held my tongue during the two or three hours that had just passed, ever since we'd left the Malakassian Dormitory.

We were alone in the city under torrents of rain. She walked with long athletic strides without taking my own speed into account. I had a very hard time keeping up with her. The distance between us grew longer and longer and I often got the impression I'd lost her, and then I would perceive her through the rain, leaning against a tree, pretending to think and, in reality, waiting for me. I was valuable to her in the maze of the camp, where the compounds looked too much alike to be useful as landmarks to a tourist. I'd lost all illusions regarding our relationship. I'd grasped that the mad love that had lit up my life thirty years ago would now and forever be reduced to nothing but the accessories and remnants of youth. I was wise enough to be contented with the sort of forbearance she showed me, even if, at the same time, this forbearance was marked by constant anger and, for my part, so as not to attract disparaging remarks, I forced myself to censure any expression of passion. I approached her, I didn't touch her despite a very strong occasional desire to do so, I restrained all my outpourings of affection, all my requests for compassionate comradery. I behaved humbly and modestly. And when I hugged a plane tree to whisper my analyses of the events taking place and to repeat some prayers and entreaties, I turned my mouth toward the depths of the bark and arranged myself so that my wretched words could not be heard. I didn't want her to take me for a weepy, whiny, lovesick man. And yet, that's what I was. Whenever she walked in front of me, I contemplated her figure with fearful nostalgia, without lust—for we hadn't reached that point—and I imagined she would turn to me, smile at me, and hold out her arms to wrap them around me in a hug. I could not manage to break the spell that had tied me to her for three dark decades.

We were on avenue Gudgul, in the middle of puddles and pitter-pattering.

She was leaning against a tree. Once again, I had been outdistanced, and she had waited for me.

I trotted up to her, breathless.

"Hey, Breton," she asked. "What's your Chinese horoscope sign? Slug or snail?"

Breton stammered something. He was too out of breath for his panting to come out as words.

"Fuck, are you ever slow!" she declaimed.

"I've gotten older," Breton babbled at last, hoarsely.

"Even the dead manage better than you," she said scornfully.

I couldn't breathe anymore. I nodded sadly, waving a hand in front of my face to fan myself or to announce a coming objection but one that, after several seconds, did not come.

I reached out my arm to touch the tree under which she'd posted herself to wait for me. In this way I regained my balance, undermined by my wobbly legs, but I also wanted to ask the plane tree for urgent help, a little of its tranquility and strength. Despite the branches and leaves, the rain throttled us.

At present, we were finished with those eccentric outfits; we were wearing transparent raincoats with hoods that we could close with a drawstring. We'd requisitioned them in the Malakassian Dormitory and they protected us well and simply. Rebecca Rausch had wedged her sawed-off shotgun between her armpit and her thigh, which gave her the look of an avenger on a mission. As far as we were concerned, Breton and I, I had the impression we mostly looked like tourists far adrift from their campground, having lost their bicycles and any joie de vivre.

I don't know why our pause under the tree persisted. Rebecca Rausch showed no intention of moving on in the immediate future. Around us, the pools sputtered, avenue Gudgul was fuzzy. Breton had caught his breath. Emboldened perhaps by this moment of relative quietude, he took the liberty of offering his opinion on Rebecca Rausch's plan of action.

"No point in going to the House of Cosmonauts," he suggested.

"That's where we're going," Rebecca Rausch said, contradicting him.

I immediately reproached myself for having opened my mouth but, feeling a kind of anxious emptiness welling up inside me, I insisted:

"There's nothing of interest for you there," Breton insisted.

"The cellar," said Rebecca Rausch.

"Nothing but interrogation cells there," said Breton. "I know the place. That's where we were beaten by Kaytel and his minions."

"You don't know anything, Breton," Rebecca Rausch hissed. "What about the metal cupboards in the boiler room? There are cupboards with weapons in the boiler room."

"Never saw 'em."

Rebecca Rausch shrugged.

"Is it far?" she asked.

"The cupboards?" Breton suggested.

"The cosmonauts," whispered Rebecca Rausch.

"Two streets away," said Breton. "Two more streets and two more compounds."

We began walking again. The city was deserted, so we advanced without observing the slightest military protocol. There was as much water on the sidewalks as on the roadway, the water bubbled all around us. The raindrops resounded on our hoods. The rain had intensified over the past hour and the streets were treacherous fords. Already more than once I'd found myself mired to mid-calf in a cold bath. I extracted myself from these traps with as little noise as possible, hoping that Rebecca Rausch had not noticed my misadventures. She had a warrior's instinct so keen that she never fell into invisible holes as I did.

She proceeded with self-assurance, here and there moving left or right to avoid obstacles that I couldn't make out. I tried to follow in her exact footsteps. Wasted effort. Every hundred steps or so I would find myself soaked to the bones, plural: tibia and fibula, not to mention the tarsus.

Then the sinister façade of the House of Cosmonauts loomed in front of us. I pushed the heavy door, stepping aside to allow Rebecca Rausch to go in.

Returning here brought up too many emotions in me. I ran to a corner of the corridor and doubled over to vomit. Breton imitated me immediately. Several burps, a continuous filament of drool that connected my mouth to the ground. To the marble slabs, fleecy with old dust.

When I'd finished my lamentable little business and stood straight up again, my legs rubbery and a horrid taste on my tongue, I realized that Rebecca Rausch hadn't waited for me and had disappeared toward the cellar.

I hung around for a moment in the half-light. The rain could be heard crackling and humming outside, against the walls and the high windows of the corridor. I had no desire to go down to the cellars. I had no recollection of the cupboards Rebecca Rausch had spoken about. What I did recall, however, is that I was dragged down there to be shoved around, terrorized, and interrogated.

Doors were furiously slammed down below, then the sound of footsteps. Rebecca Rausch was coming back up. She hadn't even reached the top step when she called to me.

"Fuck! Nothing but false information!" she cried.

"Fuck those fucking stupid photos!" she cried. "The boiler room, okay, but not a single cupboard."

I would have liked to remind her that I'd been right about the cupboards, but as she was vociferating I was submerged under a wave of nausea and I had to pivot to turn my back to her. Spasms. Nothing reached my mouth, no fetid liquid, but I was doubled over, tense, my whole body aching, my stomach churning, and suddenly I didn't give a damn about making a nasty comment regarding my excellent knowledge of the House of Cosmonauts.

Behind me, Rebecca Rausch was ranting and raving.

"Years and years of training using shitty documents! We were sent to the frontline with the crazies! They lied about our survival chances! Fucking fucked-up trainers! Fucking fuckers of the black space!"

I had a final hiccup, and then approached her. A minute passed, silent and still. Rebecca Rausch stopped speaking. She controlled her rage.

"Come on, let's go somewhere else," she growled at last, temperately.

"Look for the others," she added.

She thumped my shoulder. A sign of soldierly complicity. Nothing could have made me happier. It was as if she were officially naming me an auxiliary combatant. Together we would find the others. Together we would put the revolution and the Party back on track, reestablish the basic ideological norms and liquidate all imposters.

I would have liked to slam the heavy door to the corridor on our way out. Rebecca Rausch passed me and rushed outside under the howling deluge. The door responded much too slowly to my pulling. Already Rebecca Rausch was sloshing in great strides down the avenue. She brandished her shotgun, ready to fire, and I had the sense she was fighting against the desire to shoot randomly into the diluvian emptiness in front of her. I refrained at the last second from calling to her to beg her to wait for me and, since I didn't want to be left behind, the door remained ajar as I raced headlong into the downpour.

47

Endless rain.

Squalls that blew at us slantwise, sideswiped us.

Sound of water whipping all surfaces, streaming.

Trees spitting back as much rain as they got, mutant plane trees, velvet-apple acacias, big-eared lindens, well-bred lindens, Darling chestnut trees, fig trees. They're dumping rain in buckets.

Muddy rivers along the rows of trees.

And no one anywhere.

The places where hebephreniacs would stroll—completely empty, deserted by their silly, autistic, or bizarre shadows.

Nary a silhouette walking, or paralyzed with fear, or meditating.

Not the slightest animal or madman, not the least veterinarian, guard, or minion.

The entire landscape nothing but the translucent immensity of the rain.

Thus we wandered for several half hours, one behind the other. The distance between us increased or decreased according to Breton's fatigue and mood. Then we joined up under an acacia and Rebecca Rausch asked me if we would soon reach our goal. Until then, she'd simply indicated to me the sector toward which she wanted me to lead her. She wanted to go toward the southwest, all the way to the Shigatse sector. Now she was giving me an exact address. A ward on boulevard Yamamachvili. I should have thought of it sooner. It was obvious. The Maternity Palace. Where the Central Committee would meet at critical moments and where, according to her, the Monroe girls must have already gathered for the final offensive.

"We've passed boulevard Yamamachvili," Breton announced with the self-assurance of an infallible scout.

"Fucking shitty stupid maps!" Rebecca Rausch commented. "Months and months to memorize them, and everything was wrong!"

During the next fifteen minutes, it was she who followed my lead. I could hear her plashing in the water behind me and from time to time I'd turn around. She looked stressed and in a bad mood.

The rain was winding down and, after a few intense rallies, ceased.

We'd arrived at boulevard Yamamachvili—an endless series of administrative buildings with identical façades of a greenish gray that the downpour had refreshed. It was a sector I knew only from hearsay. You needed to present a special authorization that I didn't have and, above all, you needed to want to rub shoulders with power. Access was blocked on the side streets by militia men belonging, in all probability, to a species somewhere between humans, aliens, and Komodo dragons. I'd never tried to break through their roadblocks. Rebecca Rausch drew up to my level when we approached the first checkpoint. She shouldered her sawed-off shotgun like a fighter ready for battle, a posture greatly facilitated by the fact that it was no longer raining and she could have her raincoat wide open. But no target. There was no one at the control posts, no minion—high-powered or otherwise—no militia man, half-alien or not. Like the rest of the camp, the place was deserted.

"Cora Kliff and Mirka Goldenberg have already begun the work," Rebecca Rausch commented. "Viola Mourmansk and Marian Magadane must be in the forefront with Lola Schnittke. For all we know, the Central Committee has already been liquidated."

"Bah," I said at random.

"We are the Monroe girls," Rebecca Rausch proclaimed bizarrely, as if microphones were being held up to her and she had to explain the situation to unknown listeners.

I looked at her humbly, waiting for what was to come next.

"We obey Monroe and we do what we have to."

We'd passed the checkpoint, the sky was growing brighter, the world around us was made of tinkling raindrops and singing pipes and, although there was no audience except for us, she made a declaration of general policy. I think it had been composed to recite before the final offensive and she deemed it was time to take the floor to convince the masses of the validity of the current action.

"Workers, peasants!" she began. "Obscure members and members of no rank of the hospital personnel. Mental dissidents! Organic dissidents! Earthlings without a party and survivors! Schizophrenics and patients treated like cattle! Misguided torturers! Futureless thugs! Ordinary Party sympathizers! Dead soldiers! Living dead!"

Because I recognized myself in a few of the categories she was reeling off, I went to sit quietly in front of her, on a cement milestone that was wet but at the right height. I was pleased that someone, in a solemn speech, was taking into account the existence of people like me. Breton hesitated for ten seconds then sidled up beside me.

"She's raving," he whispered.

"Shut up," I instructed.

"She's closing her eyes while spouting inanities," he whispered again.

"Shut up," I repeated nervously. "You never understood the language of the Party."

"And you did?" he asked.

"No, neither did I," I admitted. "But stop wriggling around. Don't disrupt the meeting."

"There's no one listening to her," continued Breton.

I pointedly turned away from him.

After she'd drawn up the long list of her interlocutors, Rebecca Rausch began her actual speech to the masses. Breton was exhausted by the walk and dozed off at the first words. As for me, I squinted as if the light falling from the sky dazzled me, but it was to hide my deep desire to close my eyes and not open them again. An uncontrollable drowsiness had come over me. I forced myself to grasp the main points of Rebecca Rausch's speech, but I must confess that a large part of it escaped me. She called on the masses to approve a new direction for the Party, now restructured under Monroe's leadership, and to finish the great cleansing of the cowards, bureaucrats, opportunists, and traitors by hunting them down in their dens or by exposing them if they were disguised as hospital workers, hybrid creatures, or patients. For a few moments difficult to measure, I tried to imagine what she meant by hybrid creatures, what one could possibly imagine in this category, then I wondered if perhaps I'd misinterpreted her words and with that my thoughts drifted away. Her speech continued and above all I had to avoid snoring, which would have been insulting to the speaker. Whatever it takes, mustn't fall asleep, I thought. Mustn't act like that boor Breton, who was openly nodding off. Above all mustn't show the speaker that her call to the masses puts the masses to sleep.

I stood up. I was swaying like a sleepwalker.

Rebecca Rausch had just finished her harangue. Her eyes still had something feverishly epic about them, she was still under the spell of exaltation. Immediately I pretended to have been galvanized like the rest of the public.

"Enough words," she continued in a voice that remained vibrant and vibrating. "Time to go now!"

We headed toward the Maternity Palace, where a century earlier the authorities had moved their headquarters after the fire in the Government Center.

The rain was nothing but a memory. We had stopped dripping and we were advancing splashingly and bravely on boulevard Yamamachvili, sometimes causing small sprays, sometimes walking on surfaces that seemed barely damp. The air temperature had found its usual level, its usual slightly suffocating mildness. Perhaps because he was unfamiliar with these places where he'd never wandered, or perhaps because he had the impression he was heading toward a final lap, Breton did not let himself lag behind. Sometimes he even managed to catch up to Rebecca Rausch to the point of flanking her on the left, obviously only for fleeting moments, but flanking her nonetheless. Then we arrived in front of the Maternity Palace.

Columns. A huge fan-shaped staircase with a good fifteen steps. An imposing gateway of sculpted wood representing heroic mothers. A smaller door for daily comings and goings, which in principle you couldn't go through without showing your credentials to an orderly. A guard in uniform or a minion in plain clothes should have been in the gatehouse. There was no one and, when we had climbed the stairs, we pushed open the door and went in. The entrance hall was in chaos, with boxes piled up or flipped over, furniture, documents scattered on the floor amid trails of sawdust, straw and plaster debris, as if someone were moving house. Rebecca Rausch went to dig around among the boxes to see if there were cartridge cases or traces of blood, or hidden corpses that wished us harm. As for me, I sniffed hard. It seemed to me that the place was filled with the odor of devastation. That's what came to my mind and I couldn't find another term to attach to what I was smelling.

"The place reeks of devastation," I whispered.

"That's exactly what it is," Breton confirmed quietly.

Rebecca Rausch continued to forage about. She was some twenty steps away from us and suddenly something disagreeable, extremely disagreeable and alarming, crossed my mind.

Wait, I thought. What if it were coming from her?

What? What's coming? thought Breton.

The smell, I thought. That smell of devastation. What if it's coming from her?

Stop thinking shit, Breton replied.

"What're you saying, Breton?" Rebecca Rausch screamed at us.

She'd sprung up among the piles of boxes with the surprising speed of a predatory beast, clearly very unhappy with the thought she had read in us from afar. I don't know why, perhaps because of the play of the light—for she was backlit—or because she had taken advantage of this minute of searching through the disorder of the corridor to metamorphose, I had trouble recognizing her.

I backed up against a wall, as if she were preparing to shoot at me.

It wasn't as if she were threatening me with her shotgun, but almost. And yes, alas, I have to say, she had changed.

She was not the same, she didn't even match the recent image I'd had of her while we were entering the last stretch of our odyssey on boulevard Yamamachvili. Under her transparent raincoat, she'd become hunched, shrunken, she'd shriveled and blackened, she was cardboardy in some places and sooty in others. Bumps and bizarre boney limbs appeared almost everywhere on her organism. Her body gave the impression of not being structured around a normal skeleton. On her forehead, above her right eye, a shiny urchin had formed. At the moment I had difficulty identifying her face.

"Fuck, you stupid idiot, the odor of devastation is the odor of the black space!"

"I know," I whispered, mortified.

"Nothing else to say," she shouted.

I signaled to her that I agreed and that I hadn't thought anything bad about her, then I turned around and, holding my stomach or ribs, I began to hiccup. A brownish trickle, thick and sticky, was coming out of my mouth without managing to reach the floor.

"What do you think we girls are, asshole?" she scolded as she walked toward me. "We're nothing but shitty soldiers in the service of Monroe! If we don't smell like roses you shouldn't be shocked, fucking fuck!"

I hadn't finished vomiting. I turned ninety degrees and made a conciliatory gesture.

"Shit, Breton, who are you to judge us?" she shouted again.

"I'm not judging anyone," retorted Breton with a shiver. "We're together to the end. Where you go, I go."

"So stop thinking shit," Rebecca Rausch said, calming down.

She'd just taken off her transparent raincoat. She tossed it behind her and it flew toward the boxes. Now she looked like one of those black creatures Breton and I had observed when we were on duty at our bedroom window. One of the Monroe girls, exactly the same as when she was born on rue Dellwo, an undefinable creature of Monroe's, neither living nor dead nor hybrid, on a mission among the last of the insane—not necessarily human really—even if, under her black clothes, she had a certain resemblance to a spider or a female soldier.

"Take that off, too," she recommended. "If we're going to a meeting to see the Party heads, with your plastic hood and cape, you'll definitely look like a jerk."

I let my useless raincoat slide to my feet.

"We're going to see the leaders?" I ventured.

"If they're there, we'll see them," Rebecca Rausch confirmed.

She seemed to have no doubts about what was going to take place here, in the Maternity Palace. The locale posed no problem to her, she was orienting herself here without the slightest hesitation, clearly she'd already explored it in photos or on detailed plans. She was headed toward one of the four rooms that opened onto the corridor. She was walking quickly, I wouldn't say with a military gait since now the shape of her body was bizarre, both her body and her limbs. A lively step. The odor of devastation had grown stronger around her, a halo of panicked abandonment, of death, of grilled meat, of dark emptiness, of collapse; I was trying to erase all traces of commentary in my mind out of fear that, once again, she would intercept my thoughts telepathically and take offense.

I followed her. I was near her.

While I was expecting to head toward the upper floors where, in general, the commanding authorities choose to establish themselves, instead we turned off toward a small stairway leading to the cellar.

"We're going to the basement?" Breton asked humbly.

The echo of our footsteps resounded in the stairwell, which was middlingly lit inasmuch as some of the neon tubes worked intermittently or not at all. Rebecca Rausch was holding her weapon as if she were preparing for an unpleasant encounter. She waddled as she walked and noisily slammed her feet on the floor as if she wanted to hide a lack of balance. I'd never seen her with this gait, except perhaps on rue Dellwo when she'd just fallen from the top of the building, when she'd let go of the ledge where she'd remained suspended after leaving the world of the dead.

"First, I consult with my comrades," she said over her shoulder. "We have a meeting in the midwife room, room zero zero sixteen.

"Fine," I said. "Meeting at the midwives."

"Room zero zero sixteen," she repeated for herself.

"Rendez-vous point," she explained for Breton.

"Can I be with you?" I asked.

"We accept auxiliaries."

The wide, endless hallway was painted light yellow. Rebecca Rausch froze in front of the double door marked with the numbers zero zero sixteen.

48

The midwives' room was divided into two sections separated by nothing—a lounge area for resting, socializing, and tea drinking, with two deep armchairs and a sofa and, beyond it, for difficult nights, half a dozen hospital beds with all their linens.

In the armchair closest to the entrance, a sprawling figure could be made out in battle dress that had been lacerated in several spots; the face was smooth and black, as if dissolved in shiny black matter. The hands and flesh that appeared in the tears exhibited skin bristling with spines, more mineral than animal and, in any case, with nothing human about it. The bald head of this creature was thrown back. There was no gaze to be found there. Farther along on the beds, other shapes were lying motionless, a pile of thorny flesh and paralyzed faces, rigid, and sometimes, in place of a nose, a dark gray crater. All were stiff, resembling hard wax mannequins carelessly dressed and tossed in the dormitory with a glaring absence of compassion.

I was immediately assaulted by a powerful odor of devastation and death. The stench of burnt charcoal and sick tissue filled the air. Aware that I was merely an auxiliary who was no doubt unwelcome, I refrained from expressing what was going through my mind and, since I was perhaps under Rebeca Rausch's telepathic surveillance, I tried hard not to think of anything. I let out no cry of terror, I showed none of my disgust. I slid into a corner with the intention of moving and vomiting there as little as possible.

Next to me, Breton was scared stiff.

Rebecca Rausch went over to the armchair and the creature sprawled there.

"Mirka Goldenberg," she said. "Is that you?"

"Yes," she responded.

Mirka Goldenberg, I thought. One of the Monroe girls. I saw her being born on rue Dellwo. She was in great shape then. How could she have wound up like that?

"What happened?" asked Rebecca Rausch.

"Nothing went as planned," said Mirka Goldenberg.

Mirka Goldenberg moved no part of her body, not even her lips, but from this inert mass, from this mouth frozen under a sort of black resin, an almost normal voice emerged. A bit slow, a bit nasal, but normal. She recounted in a few sentences the catastrophic aftermath of the events that had led the Monroe girls to room zero zero sixteen, not to celebrate a historic success, but to perish horribly and metamorphose into dead women.

The girls had regrouped as agreed in their plan of action, they had taken note of Lilia Adouldjamani's and Rebecca Rausch's absence, and, without waiting for them, they'd gone to gun down the enemies of the people who had taken over the Party for much too long and occupied the Central Committee unjustifiably. The girls had scattered throughout the Maternity Palace and they had observed, like everywhere else in the camp, that the world was now empty, totally devoid of its inhabitants, whether dead or alive. No one in the meeting rooms, in the offices, no one in the areas set up as panic rooms, no one in the bathrooms. Without having shot a single bullet, they'd found themselves in the conference room where, according to their information, directors, leaders, and party heads were in session night and day. They had gone in. The room was vast, orderly, with a long central table and comfortable chairs arranged around it. A thick layer of dust, a musty smell. No gathering of leaders had been held there for eons. Installed along the wall were sound systems and recording equipment, now coated with an age-old crust dating from at least a century ago.

They had conferred. In the opinion of Cora Kliff and others, they had wandered down the wrong road since the beginning. They had left rue Dellwo and entered a side street by mistake. Perhaps they had entered a parallel universe that resembled the psychiatric camp but in reality they were swimming elsewhere, in the middle of a nightmare, in a dense dream, with no Party and no way out.

Viola Mourmansk had gone to check out the piles of equipment and among the gear had unearthed a radio transmitter for cosmonauts and the dead. She had turned it on and the girls had immediately established contact with Monroe. The connection was good. Monroe paid no attention to their report. He'd interrupted them from the first negative descriptions. He hadn't listened to the doubts they were expressing. He had commanded them to return to room zero zero sixteen and wait there. He was coming. He was coming to sort things out. And with that, the connection was cut. During a second attempt, the thing crackled and whistled in a ghastly manner, and afterward Monroe's voice was never audible again.

They had shut off the radio and withdrawn to the midwives' room. And there, in less than half an hour, they'd begun to degenerate organically, to be covered with spines and resin. One after the other they passed away. Without horrible suffering and without theatrics, Mirka Goldenberg explained.

"But without tenderness," she whispered.

Then she was silent.

Rebecca Rausch waited a handful of seconds then coughed up a short sentence with an intonation somewhere between a question and a grief-stricken statement.

"Monroe, he's coming," she half-queried.

She showed no compassion for Mirka Goldenberg or the other girls already stiffened on the beds in the second half of the room and resembling enormous, dismantled insects contaminated with inhuman, urchin illnesses. I hadn't stopped vomiting. I felt very weak. I'd had enough. Breton had moved away, he was doubled over, hiccupping as well. Our two nauseas, like the passing of the girls, were without theatrics but without tenderness. As much as the revolting odor of devastation, Rebecca Rausch's indifference made us ill at ease. She had been trained to react without panicking to the most disastrous situations. But we had not.

"They lied to us," murmured Mirka Goldenberg again. "Our survival expectancy was unpredictable, and in reality was extremely short. All they did was lie to us. Monroe is a fucking bastard like the rest of them."

"He'll come sort things out," Rebecca Rausch said to calm things down.

Of all of the Monroe girls assembled in the room she was by far the most valiant. Although I was shocked by her lack of empathy for her comrades, I was proud that the love of my life was the best survivor among all the dead girls. I wanted to tell her and I turned to her, after having negotiated a final retch. That's when I noticed on her neck, between her clavicle and her jaw, a large spiny black protuberance.

She, too, was degenerating, I thought. Her flesh is becoming or re-becoming nightmarish.

Perhaps I'd thought too loudly. Rebecca Rausch glared at me.

"Fuck, Breton!" she roared. "Keep your fucking judgments to yourself."

"Who is that guy?" asked Mirka Goldenberg, as if she had only just noticed my presence.

"I don't really know," said Rebecca Rausch. "A crazy wandering around the area. A sort of survivor. He was collaborating with both the police and Monroe."

"I saw you both being born," I ventured.

"You see?" said Rebecca Rausch, shrugging her shoulders that were becoming ever more dislocated. "He's a poor insane asshole."

The two girls lost interest in me. They continued to converse without moving their lips, no doubt by telepathy, or else they were content to stay face to face while waiting for one of them to breathe her last.

I went over to the door and to Breton, who was leaning against the door frame, breathing irregularly, almost sobbing. When I was right next to him, he whispered to me that the Party was fucked, and we were too, and that the world was going to come to an end.

"What? What's going to come to an end?" I asked, not sure I had heard correctly.

"Shut up, Breton," he whispered. "It's fucked."

We leaned despondently against one another. A few steps away, the two Monroe girls had begun their dialogue again aloud and in an unintelligible voice. The sounds that came out of their mouths were grating and interrupted by silences during which all that remained was a screeching background noise. Their words stretched out or fell apart. I can't describe exactly what was happening to their language. The words fell apart, I can't say it better than that. Some syllables, in the middle of a murmur, became strident. The silences formed bizarre strings and, deep down, I believe these silences had meaning.

"Do you understand the language of the dead?" Breton asked in an almost imperceptible whisper.

"That of the recent dead or that of the long dead?" I asked for clarification.

"Either," said Breton in a very soft voice.

"No," I said in the same tone.

Then the girls separated. Very slowly and with great difficulty, Mirka Goldenberg got up and moved toward the beds, toward an empty bed onto which she crumpled. Her limbs spread out revoltingly, independently of the bones that should logically have provided joints. Now she was only a doll made of doll fragments, covered with black blotches and urchins that had torn her clothes to shreds. Rebecca Rausch followed her with her eyes as she walked; then, when Mirka Goldenberg had crumbled hideously, she took her place in the armchair. She sat down gracelessly and, with the movements of a handicapped zombie, curled up. The top of her jacket and her pants had burst under the pressure of the black and horribly spiny blisters. Her face was lacquered, fixed under some fabric that no longer had anything but a very distant relation to skin. Obviously, I no longer recognized the face that had haunted me my entire life in the camp, and that I had never stopped waiting for, fantasizing about, and loving.

"Rebecca," I ventured.

"Don't snivel, Breton," she snarled.

Once again, she was pronouncing words in a language I could understand.

"Get in contact with Monroe," she continued. "Tell him about us. He'll make the other girls come. The Party needs to be saved."

"Bah," I declared.

"Even if you wind up all alone, save the Party. Even if you're the last one."

Her words: a final inaudible sigh, in living language, but maybe she was attempting to accompany those words with a telepathic message. I had trouble hearing them and they were coming in somewhere besides my eardrums. And then she was no longer moving her lips, totally imprisoned in a mixture of tar and resin, immobilized.

"We'll do our best," I assured her.

49

For ten minutes or so, we didn't really know what to do. Breton's opinion was to lay out Rebecca Rausch's remains so as to make it seem she'd died of natural causes, to make her look like a normal deceased loved one but, at the same time, he was loath to approach her and manipulate her. As for me, I proposed abandoning the Monroe girls in their zero zero sixteen tomb, to shut off the light behind us, close the door and then, together, do our best to reform or save the Party. These ten minutes were used to stand up with minimal wobbling and to pray. We touched the wood of the door attempting to imagine it was still a living tree and not a cutout from a corpse. We excused ourselves to the tree in the name of humanity and, more precisely, in the name of the survivors in the camp and in the name of the Party, but the main prayer was a faint whispering about the end of the world, followed by an inquiry about the reality of the death of every man and woman and about the imminence of our own death, Breton's and mine. It was, I confess, a bumbling inquiry interrupted by sobs. A trickle of spittle and snot dripped slowly toward our shirtfront. As our discourse to the wood panel was becoming more and more incoherent, we agreed to end it.

In front of us, Rebecca Rausch was nothing more than a mass sprinkled with black bumps bristling with spikes. She had gone back to where she'd come from and left as a souvenir an envelope that was unbearable to look at.

Without hanging around, we shut off the lamps in the midwives' premises and, having closed the door behind us, we walked away. In the corridor, the odor of devastation was not as strong. We felt exhausted and walked slowly, with pauses during which we leaned on a wall waiting for a spasm that sometimes came, sometimes not.

Soon we were in the entrance hall. Night had fallen, the erratic piles of boxes and chairs looked like a barricade. We were about to leave the building when Breton decided otherwise.

"What will we do outside?" he spluttered.

We turned around. The room was poorly lit by a streetlamp from the avenue—a random dark room. The stairs. We climbed the steps laboriously to the second floor, then to the third. A long hallway ended in darkness. We plunged into it; from time to time we felt doorknobs under our hands. Offices, bedrooms, who knows. Everything was locked. Halfheartedly we tried to open them, then we walked farther along.

At the end of the hallway, one door gave way. We entered a rather large bedroom, furnished with two box springs, two mattresses, and two chairs. There were also night tables and a dismantled wardrobe. Breton worked the switch, a ceiling lamp lazily lit, dispensing a light equal to that of one candle, then two. The bedroom was equipped with a small bathroom with a shower and a toilet. The window gave onto a street without trees. I peered outside.

"It looks like rue Dellwo," Breton remarked.

Tram tracks, electric cables that formed ugly nets at the height of the second floor, façades soaked by rain, windows in bad shape, black, hiding absence, dilapidation, the non-existence of inhabitants since the end, or even the beginning, of time.

"Well we don't need Hirsch glasses to see what's happening," I said.

Breton reflected for a moment before commenting.

"Not sure anything is happening," he stated.

I pulled a chair over to the window and sat down. Breton went to shut off the ceiling lamp. The same light continued to fall from it.

A moment. An immeasurable moment.

"It's started raining," Breton noted after this moment.

In order to fight against dozing off, I proposed beginning a game of chess without a chessboard, in our heads, but Breton talked me out of it. We were neither in a state or in the mood to throw ourselves into such an adventure.

"Might as well let the hours go by," he suggested.

We settled as close to the window as possible with the intention of keeping an eye out, remaining vigilant so that nothing would escape us. The landscape was immobile. The gutters spit little torrents directly on the sidewalks. Every fifty meters, the streetlamps lit the soot of the puddles and façades. It wasn't raining very hard, but the rain dripped noisily on everything. Our priority was to watch the windows of the highest floors. Some still had their glass panes, others had been closed with boards.

For hours I had been on the verge of collapse. I could no longer even hold my breath. From time to time, I would stand and, rocking from side to side, I'd arrive over the toilet bowl, not knowing really if I should urinate or vomit; then, having done or pretended to do the one and the other, I would go back to sit on the chair. We no longer exchanged the slightest sentence, Breton and I. When Breton would leave his post to go to the bathroom in turn, he would lean on me or brush my shoulder in comradery, but without saying anything.

In this way a good part of the evening and night passed when suddenly Breton perceived a movement at the window of the most dilapidated house among all those facing us, on the fifth floor.

"Something," he said.

"Something or someone," I said.

The window had no pane, only a portion of its structure had survived its own decrepitude. A rotund form, half dressed, had just pushed out what remained of it. This form was pulling itself out of the black room, without confidence, evoking none of the acrobatic flexibility of the Monroe girls. It was no longer one of the Monroe girls.

"It's Monroe," said Breton.

I wasn't so sure, but I didn't contradict him.

We couldn't make out the number of limbs emerging from that vaguely spherical mass but, because it was more or less covered in clothes, we had to admit that it wasn't an animal. Organically, nothing was definable. But let's say Monroe. By process of elimination, it could only be Monroe. He was trying to leave the world of the dead to come to the rescue of the girls he'd sent on mission earlier.

"It can only be him," Breton said.

"Him or one of his minions," I said.

"Let's say it's him," Breton decided.

I acquiesced. The unnamable or barely nameable creature was at the moment suspended over the void, hanging from the window ledge. The rain was lashing it and since it had remained without moving for a moment it was beginning to drip fiercely.

"He doesn't look particularly at ease," I remarked.

"He didn't get the training the girls got," said Breton. "He's discovering how it feels to leave the space of the dead and enter the nightmare of the living."

"Yeah," I added. "It's his turn to see it now."

For half an hour, Monroe remained motionless at the fifth floor, holding on to the window. He held fast. We couldn't see if he was using all his members to cling there, or how many he possessed, four or six or more. He didn't have a human form.

"That happens when you slide too quickly from one world to the other," I commented.

We didn't feel much compassion for Monroe.

"He should have prepared himself better," said Breton.

Half an hour, then another. The rain beat down. At the end of the street canyon, the tracks were disappearing beneath the water.

I got up again to vomit in the toilet. Nothing came out of my mouth. I persisted, then had the impression that, in my state, it was pointless to vomit or urinate.

"Why do you think that?" Breton questioned me telepathically.

"Fuck you, Breton," Breton quoted to give me a little courage.

I went back to sit down. I didn't really know if I had stopped breathing or was panting.

On the façade of the old house, on the fifth floor, Monroe had disappeared.

He disappeared? I asked.

He let go, Breton thought.

I left the chair to see the street, the sidewalk. Monroe had crashed there. A pool of black liquid surrounded him and he wasn't moving. I remained with my forehead stuck against the glass, waiting for him to emerge from his fainting spell. If he had been knocked out at the end of his fall, there would certainly be a moment when he would return to life. We had trouble imagining that he would not get up again. We were many to await his coming. Many men and many women. We had trouble imagining that he would have gone through the abominable passage between death and the world of the living only to find himself immediately in the position of a defenestrated corpse.

I began to stutter a few prayers in a whisper, then was silent. The rain pounded, the image no longer changed, the tram tracks simmered under a black layer, Monroe was absolutely no longer moving, he resembled a bag of charcoal abandoned in the water. There were still hours and hours to go before morning. Let's say three hours. In the middle of the third, Breton pronounced a judgment for which I hold him entirely responsible.

He botched his debut in the camp, he thought.

In the camp or in life, I ventured.

Well we'd better not botch our end, Breton continued in thought.

The end of what? I asked.

No one answered. Breton had fallen asleep. I did the same.

VII

Annex

The 343 Factions of the Party in its Glory Days
The Awful Beggars
The Black Bonnets
The Reconstituted Proletarian Opposition
The Leninists of the Fifth Day
The Flag
The Trotsko-Absolutists
The Monroe-Absolutists
The Servants of the Ninth Thesis
The "Maxillo-Facial Surgery" Department
The Assembly of Anti-Capitalist Thanatologists
The Reconstituted Faces
The Neo-Councilists
The Amateur Bundists
The Bundists of Radiant Radicality
The Black Alliance
The Polpotist Tolerance
The Posadists of the Ninth Month
The Unified Bordigists
The Neo-Pavlovians
The "Obdurate" Faction
Bronstein's Men
The Men from Kronstadt
The Seven Women of the Liberation
The Zoophile Quintet
The Intercontinental Red Army
The Marxists of Great Compassion

The Scarlet Pavilion
The Everything-but-Monroe
The "Guillotine" Faction
The Black Widows' Door
The Brothers-in-Arms
The Absolute Sisters of the Third Manifesto
The Rendez-Vous Dwarves
The Majoritarian Insurrectionalists
The Proletarian Samurais
The "Tomorrow the Orcas" Faction
The Eleven Disciples
The Final Unity
The Horse Butcher
The Return-to-Fundamentals
The Disappointed by Polpotism
The Low Ebb
The Women of the Eighth Crossing
The Power to the Soviets
The Mothers of the Great Night
The Neo-Oncologists
The "Old Shotgun" Leaning
The Voice-of-the-People
The Rebels of the Apocalypse
The Communist She-Dogs
The Communists of April 25
The Virgins-with-Child
The Society of Insubordinates
The Miners of the Great Night
The Eternal Workers
The Diamond Revolution

The Partisans of the Red Lotus
The Vermillion Dissidence
The "Retribution" Leaning
Frankenstein's Fiancées
The Rita Manchukuos
The Awakening of the Day Before
The Autonomous of the Bardo
The Egalitarians of the Small Vehicle
The Reconstituted Bindlestiffs
The "Infectious Diseases" Section
The Still and Forever Unrepentant
The Red Notebook
The Children of Communism
The Very-Red Damsels
The Unified Factions
Radical Stomatology
The Revolutionaries of the End
The Blissful Shambles
The Coal Trimmers of the Final Victory
The "Day After"
"The Baabar Perspective" Leaning
The Brave Soldiers
The "Baba Yaga Perspective" Leaning
The Proletarian Revenge
The Empty Sky Way
The Soldiers of Value Added
The Revenants
The Night Lights of the Final Hour
The Psychomotor Assistance
The "Red Oncology" Department

The Beloved Factionists
The Revolutionary Dermatologists
The Fifteenth Battalion
The Hardline Brats
The Final Rabble
The October Threshing Machine
The Scarlet Fraternity
The "Headwind" Group
The Ushers in Front of the Door
The Reconstituted Melancholies
The Poor Men's Choice
The Itinerant Egalitarians
The Invisible Cleaners
The Silk Road
The Alumni
The Runoffs
The Celestial Sharers
The "Never Without my Kim" Leaning
The Libertarians of the Incarnation
The Right of First Refusal
The "Impermanence" Grouping
The Paramedics of January 13
The "Shoot 'em first" Faction
The Palate Cleansers
The Five Ruddy Dwarves
The "Everything Right Now" Youth
The Senior Citizen Communists
The Valiant Saboteurs
The Fish Market
The Faceless Obscure

The Adept of the Ninth Oath
The Maoists Past Their Prime
The Conformists
The "Anti-Faction" Faction
The Neo-Excursionists
The Dzerzhinskists of Great Compassion
The Next Avalanche
The Adventurers of the Third Day
The Human Tide
The Guerrilleros of the Flag
The Commune for All
The Pétroleuses and Proud of It
The Audacious Preparators
The Eleventh Commandment
The Strategic Withdrawers
The She-Wolves of the Great Duality
The She-Wolves of Non-Duality
The Communards of the Supreme Awakening
The Renewal of the Extinction
The Little People
The "Young Insurrection" Group
The Last Stand
The Lava of the Great Day
The "Strike!" Group
Proletarian Obstinacy
The Dogs of Nivôse
The "Immediate Illumination" Group
The Disciples of Bogdanov
The Pro-Forma Chekists
The Walking Fossils

The Exorcists in Ambush
The Red Hope Army
The Barrels of Laughs
The Misplaced Organs
The Four Accordionists
The Brothers Communist
The Sisters of the Red Way
The "Let's Go" Group
The Eye-Opening Blind
The Shake-up-the-Bourgeoisie Concerto
The Associated Bolsheviks
The Red Coral
The "Last Fight" Faction
The Worker's Horizon
The Violent Firewall
The Female Meditators of the Riot
The Stage Door
The Guaranteed Maximum
The Millipede's Path
The Flaming Foulards
The Operating Room
The Zero Zero Seventeens
The Unbearable Suspense
The Seven-League Boots
The Nostalgic for the Union
The Soldiers of Farewell
The Red Technicians
The Midwives of the Future
The "Never Fallen, Still Standing"
The "No Details, No Devil"

The Tar Wave Faction
The Tidal Wave Faction
The Matron Girls
The Unapologetic Leftists
The With the Grain
The "Let's Confess Everything" Tendency
The Fiddlers on the Roof
The "Pause" Movement
The Neo-deconstructionists
The Grandiose Finale
The Massacre of the Innocents
The "No Future" Alliance
The Seven Openings
The Sumptuous Factionists
Left Rudder
The Crucible
The Libertarians, Plain and Simple
The Brotherhoodly Revival
The Portside Before and After
The Interventionists of the Third Kind
The Polyglot Mutual Support Group
The Central-Central Committee
The Executed to Set an Example
The Little Match Girl
The Babouvist Illumination
The Shellfish
The Storm Warnings
The New Members
The Grassroots
The "Five Perfume" Communists

The Old Taciturns
The "Homestretch" Tendency
The "Defense of the Past"
The Ineffable Mess
The All-in-One
The Mysterious Barricades
The Technicians of the Bardo
The Sparkling Dogmatics
The Leninist Church
The Leninist Church of the First Day
The Church of Lenin the Triumphant
The New Church of Equality
The Bordigists of the Great Night
The Smokescreen
The Red Renouncers
The Devil's Pool
The "Autumn Harvest" League
The Sermonizers
The Retinal Persistence
The Partisans of Leaping into the Unknown
The Guardian Angels of Leninism
The Defenders of the Faith
The Scarlet Secret
The No-Smoking Section
The Full Split
The Bright-Light Minimalists
The Maximalists of Bedazzlement
The "Wow, Fascinating. Not!" Leaning
The Proletarian Trench

The Socialist League
The Fountain of Youth
The Advocates of Sacred Experience
The Sword Swallowers
The Hand-of-Buddha
The Weathermen
The Red Crossbills
The Purge
The Rehabilitated as a Formality
The "Give 'em an inch, they'll take a yard" contingent
The "Burial" Faction
The Defeat is Over
The Egalitarian Struggle
The Tabula Rasa
The Followers of Tradition
The Interurban Communists
The Last Stronghold
The Pot-au-Feu
The Orthodox
The Seven Grumpies
The Validation of the Accredited
The Moderate Terrorists
The Skin and Bones
The Blushing Soldiers
The Bolshevik Line
The Great-Day Conformists
The Precious Posadists
The "Lesbians without Borders"
The Companions of Defeat

The Stars of the Past
The Soldiers of Intransigeance
The "Revenge of the Zeks" Group
The Sparkling Lotuses
The Sea Walls
The One Hundred Thousand Volts
The Giap Group
The Sleeping Beauties
The Ancestral Red
The Semi-Idiots
The Libertarian Succession
The Delivery Room
The Trotskyist Apotheosis
The Front of the Penitents
The Challenge
The Take-the-Money
The Men of the Future
The "Lights over the City" Leaning
The Rampagers
The Restructuring from Below
The Religious Maniacs
The Bakers of the Eleventh Hour
The Fulfilled Baker's Wife
The "Where's the Bathroom" Movement
The Right to Scrutinize
The Inner-Suburbs Insurgents
The "Icebreaker" Leaning
The Dustbins of History
The Black Manuelas

The Chinese Takeout
The "Full Steam Ahead" Faction
The Egalitarian Renunciation
The Five Tardigrades
The Twelve Sleepy Leaders
The "Armored Train" Bloc
The Witch Alliance
The Therapy by Fire
The Peasant Renaissance
The "Nearing the Goal"
The "Gastroenterology" Ward
The New Age Proletariat
The Martian Arts
The Partisans of Defeat
The Passengers of the Small Vehicle
The "Our Great Ancestors" Leaning
The Bolsheviks of Melancholy
The "Last Vestige" Group
The "Better Never than Late"
The "Raincheck" Leaning
The Subtle Revolution
For a Revolutionary Vodou
The Saboteur Girls of Narrow Passageways
The Dazzled Militant Girls
The "Everything but a General Secretary"
The Damsels of the Telephone
The "Razor's Edge" Movement
The Wholesale Purchases
The Perfection Blazing

The First Turn to your Left
The Fight Against Plantar Warts
The "Our Dearly Beloved"
The "Pinch Me" Movement
The Warrior Monks
The Partisans of the Red Abyss
The Now and Forever Vociferators
The Four Grand Absents
The Seconds in Command of Chaos
The Alternative Flip-Floppers
The "Heavy Fire" Faction
The Star Players of the Party
The Headquarters in Reconstruction
The Russian Socks Committee
The Red Letter Day Adventists
The Proponents of the Precious Mirror
The Vindictive Revival
The "Get with the Program" Faction
The "Rescue Dinghy" Faction
The Faction "If we are thousands"
The Faction "This is the end, my friend, the end"

a r c h i p e l a g o   b o o k s

is a non-profit publisher devoted to
promoting cross-cultural exchange through innovative
classic and contemporary international literature
archipelagobooks.org

e l s e w h e r e   e d i t i o n s

translates luminous picture books from around the world
elsewhereeditions.org